Welcoming the Rain

Welcoming the Rain

A novel

Bess Hendrick

Cover art by Angela Tanabe
IG/Twitter: xinamadden

This is a work of fiction.
Any resemblance to actual persons,
living or dead, is purely coincidental.

Copyright © 2020 Bess Hendrick
ISBN 9798577494520
All rights reserved.

Inquiries: besshendrickbooks@gmail.com

Cover artwork © 2020 Angela Tanabe

Revision of Sight

I saw a sculpture once, a few years back, formed in pale clay and displayed on a table at a yoga studio among a group of objects related to the natural world. As I approached it my first impression was of a very large oyster shell with a second shell nestled inside. As I drew closer, I saw instead the ruffled edges of an orchid sitting in a narrow vase, that, no, was actually a wrist and what seemed to be the orchid, the shell, was really an open palm cradling a round object in its center. And yet, no, it was actually a woman in child's pose, her knees folded under her, her head nestled between her outstretched arms that then formed an oval, which became the edges of the shell, the orchid, the hands.

Looking at this sculpture I saw all these images, these evolving shapes, each with its own meaning, and I felt such awe. And in an odd way, I felt gratitude. You see, I was slowly losing my sight. If my vision had not been so poor would I have seen all that I did? Was what I saw in the sculpture simply a measure of the artist's depth, or misdirection caused by my failing vision? And did it really matter? Perception, after all, anybody's perception, isn't actually a stable thing, but a shifting conglomerate of sensations. We attempt to have a shared reality, a common experience of objects and events when what we're really doing is looking at a prism of perspectives, each with its own interpretation of what we are experiencing. Keeping that in mind I'm able to tell myself that my perception, the visual part of it with blurred images as fluid as an impressionistic painting, has its own validity and its own beauty. That thought helps me to be content with my out of focus world right up until the time that something happens that reminds me again of what I've lost and then I grieve for the world I once knew with its sharp edges and minute details, my ability to see the pattern on a butterfly's wing as far from my reach as the stars.

1

Poulsbo, Washington, September 2013

"Gray," she heard herself mutter and the sound of her own voice pulled Raymie back from her ruminations, over who knows what, to the rumble and sway of the bus moving toward Bainbridge Island. She ran her finger along the collected condensation on the metal rim of the rain-pocked window as they rushed past the huddled rows of dark evergreens. Everything was cold, wet, and gray.

Attuned to her every movement, her guide dog Shainy lifted her blond head from where it was resting on the knee of Raymie's faded jeans. Raymie gazed down at her fondly, and bent closer to breathe in the scent of her recent shampoo blended with the rich smell of dog.

"It's almost fall, Shainy," she told her. "But you'd think that we were already there by looking at this crummy weather, huh, girl?"

Shainy looked up at her, her brown eyes quizzical, and Raymie heard the soft thump of her tail.

There would be some lovely fall days, Raymie reminded herself, and there would be times when she could appreciate what a marvelous season autumn was, with its piles of leaves to swish through and the distant honk of geese on their flight south, but right now she was petulantly letting the gray skies that announced the coming of fall cover her like a cloak, shadowing everything with gloom.

Raymie had never thought that the rain-drenched Northwest was a good fit for her. She liked the hot, bright days of summer and imagined herself at home in some Mediterranean island, walking through narrow cobbled streets in sandals and a wide-brimmed hat.

A few years ago, shortly after Raymie's father died, her mom tried to convince her to come and live in New Mexico, where she had moved to live with Raymie's aunt. Raymie was tempted, imagining lazy afternoons on a sunny patio. But the other part of that picture, the part that she dreaded, was what it would be like living in a new town with people who didn't know her. Here in the small community where she lived, those who didn't know that she was legally blind, at least understood that she didn't see well, and were more than willing to help her out when she needed it.

Besides, the Northwest was where she was born, where her daughter and her grandson lived and where she had friends and a position with an agency that respected her competence and experience. Who would I be in New Mexico? she asked herself. Just some poor half-blind lady who lived with her aunt and widowed mother. No thanks to that!

She heard the phoosh of air brakes as the bus came to a stop followed by the sound of the ungainly double doors flapping open. Someone stepped onto the bus and started talking to the bus driver in something of a louder than normal voice. "Hi Larry! Did your kids get over the flu?"

"Yeah, Marcie," the driver answered. "Thanks for asking."

Glancing briefly at the front of the bus, Raymie saw a large square of red moving down the aisle that resolved into a woman in a red coat as she moved closer. Raymie, who wasn't in the mood for a conversation with a stranger, quickly turned her head and looked out the window to discourage company, but she heard the new passenger flop heavily into the seat across the aisle. The voice that intruded into Raymie's privacy had a friendly lilt to it.

"What's your dog's name?" The woman asked.

"Her name is Shainy," Raymie said, blending warmth with reserve, then resumed her scan of what she could see out the window. This tactic, more often than not, discouraged conversations with other riders. Raymie knew she should be more friendly. She really meant to be, but she was still pouting over having to give up her old Audi wagon, sold more than a year ago, because she could no longer drive. Where taking the bus had once been a choice, it was now a necessity, and Raymie hated to admit how much she resented that.

The other passenger ignored Raymie's hint. "It's a girl, huh?" she said. "Is she a helper dog for you? My friend Jessie has a helper dog, a guide dog, and she's blind. Jessie, I mean, not the dog." The woman giggled.

Raymie turned to get a good look at her visitor, who was sitting sideways in her seat, legs halfway into the aisle, not the way you were supposed to sit on the bus, but Raymie was grateful because she could see her better. She was a delightfully round person, with a round torso and a chubby face surrounded by a halo of dark curly hair. Her glasses were slipping down her nose and she pushed them up with one finger, turned her head to one side and gave Raymie a grin.

Suddenly charmed, Raymie smiled back at her. "Well, yes, she's a guide dog. I'm legally blind, you see, so she helps me get around, not fall off curbs and things like that."

"My name's Marcie," her visitor declared looking at Raymie expectantly.

There was a moment's hesitation. "I'm Raymie."

"Rainy?"

"No. Well, sure, why not? Rainy's alright. It rhymes with Shainy."

"Rainy and Shainy!" Marcie said, clasping her hands at her chest and smiling broadly. Raymie laughed.

Marcie leaned forward to pet Shainy, then hesitated, her eyes questioning Raymie. "Oh, yes, go ahead and pet her. I let her be off-duty while we ride."

"I don't remember seeing you on the bus before," she told Marcie.

"Oh, I ride the bus all the time. But I usually take the 6:45. My shift at Safeway was changed so now I take this bus."

Marcie moved her legs aside as a woman in a yellow raincoat walked down the aisle to take a seat in the next row back. "Hi Marcie," the passenger said as she pushed back the hood that enveloped her small gray-capped head. "You're taking a later bus than usual, aren't you?"

"I got a different shift at the store. And a raise! So now I take this bus."

"Congratulations, Marcie! I'm sure you deserve it."

Marcie set an arm on the back of her seat so she could turn more completely to the woman behind her. "What about you, Ruth? What're you up to this morning? On your way to see your mom?"

"I sure am. They're doing crafts at her nursing home and I just signed on as a volunteer so I could help out."

"Hey, that's nice of you!" There was warmth in Marcie's voice as she added, "Will you say hi to your mom for me?"

"I certainly will, sweetheart. She is always happy to know that you remember her."

Marcie turned back to Raymie. Shainy gave a little sigh, her eyes intent on Marcie, who resumed petting her.

Someone from the rear of the bus had pulled the cord to request the next stop, and as he passed by, he said, "Hey Marcie! You still bagging groceries? I'd hate to lose my favorite courtesy clerk."

"Yeah, Mike! And I got a raise."

"A raise? Way to go, Marcie."

"Thanks, Mike!" she called after him as he moved down the aisle. "Have a good day at work."

Settling herself into her seat with a movement of her shoulders, Marcie asked Raymie, "Are you going to work today too?"

"Oh, no, not today. My job is just part-time these days." She smoothed the front of her baggy sweatshirt, aware that she wasn't dressed the way she would be for work. "I'm going to spend the day at my daughter's home in Seattle."

"You take the ferry?"

"That's right. I catch the ferry and then my daughter Allison picks me up at the ferry dock," Raymie said, surprised to find herself telling this to a person that she'd just met. She'd been taught not to divulge her personal information to just anyone and was usually not so forthcoming.

"Allison? That's a pretty name."

"And I have a grandson too," Raymie added eagerly. "He's four years old."

"I'll bet he's cute!"

"He's adorable." She hesitated before asking, "Would you like to see his picture?" Inwardly she groaned. So now she was offering to let this lady see her grandson's pictures?

"Oh, yes! I'd love to see them."

Reaching into her purse, Raymie dug out her phone and gave it to Marcie, who moved over to the seat next to Raymie so she could scroll through the pictures. Raymie really couldn't see them very well, but her daughter Allison had taken the photos with Raymie's phone, saying, "You need some bragging pictures, Mom, just like every other grandma," and she was right. Whenever Raymie shared the pictures, she had the pleasure of hearing people exclaim how much Aaron looked like her, with his hazel eyes, strawberry blond hair and a few freckles across his upturned nose. Raymie was happy that he had inherited her coloring but hoped that he wouldn't end up short like she was. Only slightly more than five feet, people politely referred to her as diminutive or petite. Raymie considered it kind of them, but in the end, the truth was that she was short, plain and simple.

"I like this one best," Marcie said, leaning her head to briefly rest on Raymie's shoulder. "The one with your grandson and the cat."

Raymie chuckled, remembering how the cat squirmed every time Aaron picked him up. "Yes, he just loves that cat. I'm not so sure the cat loves him, though."

Marcie gave a little laugh, then looking up, said, "Oh! This is my stop!"

The bus pulled to the side of the road and Marcie gathered up her things. "See you tomorrow?"

"I'm looking forward to it," Raymie called after her as Marcie stepped off the bus.

The bus pulled away from the curb, leaning into traffic. As they gained speed, the drumming of rain on the roof changed pitch, then became part of a blur of sound and motion. Raymie let the rush of sound flow past her, fresh, invigorating, and yet, somehow, comforting.

The next morning Marcie slid unceremoniously into the seat next to Raymie. "Hey! Look at you!" She nodded at Raymie's attire, a long blue jacket offset by a hand-printed scarf, black pants and low-heeled boots. "Are you a teacher or something?"

"Something like that," Raymie replied, noticing how Marcie's eyes lit up with delight as she spied Shainy who was lying half hidden under the seat. "I'm a speech therapist."

Marcie's gaze returned to Raymie's face. "A speech therapist? Like someone who helps people talk better? My friend Drew used to go to a speech therapist at school. Is that what you do?"

"I've worked in schools in the past, but I don't do that these days because I can't drive anymore. Now I just see people at the clinic."

Marcie twisted her head to one side. "Did you used to help Drew? He got to leave our classroom to go to the speech therapist's office."

At such close range, Raymie could see that Marcie was older than she originally thought. She was a little jowly, with deep lines on either side of her face. "I suspect that we're close to the same age, Marcie. I was probably still in school myself when you and Drew were in class together."

"Aww, that's right!" She laughed, leaning over to give Raymie's arm a friendly push.

Shainy sat up and was scooting over, completely against her training, to beg a pat from Marcie. She looked at Raymie and gave a little whine to get her permission, and Raymie nodded to her. Shainy moved her nose close to Marcie's hand, who stroked her soft head, saying, "How are you today, beautiful girl?" Marcie glanced up at Raymie. "I was in special ed, you know."

Raymie nodded, having surmised that when she first met Marcie. "I've known a lot of people who were in Special Education classes. Did you like your teachers?"

"Yeah, they were nice and we did some fun stuff together," she said, her voice slowing and taking on a hint of sadness. "It's just that sometimes it was hard being different from the kids in the regular classes. Sometimes they made fun of kids like me and Drew."

"That sounds like it was pretty tough."

Marcie didn't respond and continued to look down at Shainy, which prompted Raymie to change to a happier subject. "You seem to have a real way with dogs. Do you have one of your own?"

She brightened immediately. "Yeah! We have Shep. He's a big old hairy thing."

"He sounds quite loveable." Curious, Raymie added, "I noticed that you said 'we' just now. Do you live with your family?"

"Oh, just with my brother Jack. My sister Jen lives in Oregon and my brother Mark lives near my parents. They moved to Palm Springs a few years ago, and my sister Lisa"—she shrugged one shoulder—"well, she died."

"I'm sorry to hear that, Marcie."

"Yeah, it still makes me sad sometimes." Marcie smoothed her hand along Shainy's back.

"I understand what it's like to lose someone," Raymie told her. "My husband died about four years ago."

"Do you still feel sad?" Marcie asked.

Did she? Raymie searched for that core of pain that she felt when he died, but couldn't find it. She felt the loneliness that comes with having a single life foisted on her after so many years of marriage, but did she specifically miss Bill? Not really. She had loved him, true, but he was a miserable man who, she would swear, could make lemons out of lemonade, always focusing on the bitter and never the sweet, and she was actually a little relieved that he was gone. "Not so much anymore," was what she chose to tell Marcie. "It gets better with time."

They were silent a moment before Raymie said, "Would you like to tell me more about your dog?"

"Shep is really sweet and he's kind of goofy too. He smiles a lot with his big tongue hanging out." She mimicked a big goofy dog, drawing her hands up to her chest to create the effect of paws, letting her tongue loll out one side of her mouth and making the panting noises people associate with a happy dog.

Raymie laughed. "He sounds like a wonderful pet."

"He is!" Marcie paused as an idea moved across her face. "I know!" she exclaimed. "You and Shainy should come and visit us! Me, Shep and Jack!"

Raymie was taken aback by the suddenness of this invitation. Not sure what to say, she finally came up with, "But we hardly know each other."

"Pish," Marcie said, mouth screwed up in a way that told Raymie she thought she was being silly. "I know you're a nice person with a nice dog. I can tell things like that. And Shep and Shainy could play together!"

Raymie was tempted. She needed to be cautious about play mates for a dog as essential as Shainy, but on the other hand, Shainy worked hard and deserved a break. "That could be fun, Marcie. But what about your brother? Wouldn't you need to check it out with him first?"

She looked puzzled. "No-o-o," she said drawing the word

out slowly. "I mean, he does what he does and I do what I do and we don't have to ask each other. We share the house, you see, but he has the apartment above the garage where he hangs out by himself a lot."

"That sounds like a comfortable arrangement. What does your brother do?"

"He reads a lot." She rolled her eyes. "Like, all the time. He teaches English at the college, poetry and stuff."

Raymie imagined a stuffy old curmudgeon with disheveled hair, his stained wool vest stretched tight over a good-sized paunch, sporting half-moon glasses, a pipe in one hand and a book in the other, droning on about some obscure passage from Paradise Lost. Amused at herself, she remembered the English Lit professor she had a crush on in her sophomore year. There'd been nothing stuffy about him.

Marcie's voice broke into her thoughts. "So, do you want to come and visit?"

"Well," Raymie said evasively, "why don't we wait a couple of weeks and reevaluate the idea then?"

"Okay!" Marcie said, nodding her head vigorously. "You'll come to visit in a couple weeks, that would be perfect!" She looked at Shainy. "You'd love to meet Shep, wouldn't you, girl?"

Raymie gave a little inward grimace. She liked Marcie and was curious about her life, but didn't feel entirely comfortable with the idea of going to her home. She didn't want to give Marcie the impression that she would be her new best friend and visit with her weekly or anything. But watching her with Shainy, who was hanging on Marcie's every gesture, every word, Raymie decided not to let herself feel uncomfortable about the invitation.

Marcie glanced up at her with an easy-going smile that

encouraged Raymie to relax. Truth be told, Raymie thought, in the short space of time she had known Marcie, what was clear was that they enjoyed each other's company. Marcie made her laugh, and her bold, carefree nature lifted her spirits like no one she'd encountered before. What better basis for a friendship?

2

"Well, glory hallelujah! Friday at last and the sun finally decided to grace us with its presence. You can't get much better than that. What do you say we blow this joint and go to the deli for lunch?"

Raymie looked up from her desk to see the lanky figure of her co-worker Julie leaning against the file cabinet opposite her desk.

"What a great idea!" Raymie motioned to Shainy, who stood up, ready to go. "Let's see if we can get a table on the deck," Raymie suggested. "It's more private there, and you'd said you wanted to talk about a problem with one of your clients."

"Yeah, that's a tricky situation, alright," Julie said, scratching the back of her neck. She dropped her arm. "And you were going to tell me about that person you met on the bus."

Julie, a good head taller than Raymie, shortened her lanky stride to match Raymie's as they walked the short distance to the deli. When they got there, they saw that the deck was deserted, just as they had hoped. It had rained the day before and the waitress hurried out with a cloth to swab up a little puddle of water that had formed at the center of the table. Clearly irritated by their request to sit on the damp but sunny deck, she plunked place settings and some menus on the table. Julie pulled out a chair, brushed bits of debris off the seat from the trees that curved over the tiny deck and slouched into it. As she took the chair across from Julie, Raymie noticed how Julie towered over her even when seated. She consciously shook off the feeling, one she often had, of being a child among adults. At least her feet didn't dangle on this chair. That was something.

Ignoring the menu, Raymie ordered her usual, the grilled chicken salad. Julie decided on a sandwich and they both ordered coffee. The waitress deposited the steaming cups in front of them with a small bowl of creams and some sugar packets. As soon as they were alone again, Julie launched into her story about a teacher who refused to let his student, Julie's speech therapy client, use a communication device in his classroom. "The damn teacher keeps saying it'll disturb the other students. Shit. I may as well be talking to a brick wall. Do you have any ideas for me?"

"Well," Raymie took an appreciative sip of her coffee, "you could always wave a copy of the boy's Educational Plan in front of the teacher's face and tell him that he must allow the device in his classroom by law."

"Yep," Julie said, "thought of that. Great way to make an enemy."

"Or," Raymie paused for effect, "you could agree with him that the device could very well cause a disturbance at first." To Julie's raised eyebrows she explained, "You see, if he feels like you're at least listening to him, maybe he will be willing to work with you in figuring out how to get the other students used to hearing the electronic voice." She chuckled. "You could even make it fun, have his classmates gather around your client and ask him questions that he can answer with the device, and maybe even have the other students try the device out for themselves."

"Hey, yeah! Those are some great ideas!" Julie said as she moved her elbows off the table to give the waitress space to put her plate down. "Thanks, Raymie. I knew that you would be the right person to ask about this."

Raymie thanked the waitress as she set her salad in front of her, then told Julie, "Please let me know how it turns out."

"I definitely will." Julie took a big bite of her sandwich. She swallowed, and holding the sandwich ready for the next bite, said, "Now what about that person you wanted to tell me about? What was her name, Marnie?"

"Marcie. She's someone I met on the bus a couple of weeks ago. She's a really nice woman about my age with a mild developmental disability." Raymie was silent a moment, remembering Marcie with pleasure. "She's a bit of a character, charming in an offbeat way and definitely funny. We've become friends of a sort. She calls me 'Rainy,' a nickname that she gave me the day we met, and I kind of like it."

"Rainy," Julie said, trying the name out. "I like it too. Kinda cute. It fits you."

"It just feels sort of odd to have a friend with a developmental disability, I guess, but we do enjoy each other's company."

Julie took a sip of her coffee, made a face and added more cream. "Not all that odd if you enjoy her company. But do you really have that much in common with her?"

Raymie tapped her mouth with her fingertips. "Well, this morning she brought in her iPod and played some of her favorite music for me. Her taste isn't altogether bad, and it turns out that she likes to dance as much as I do. She even had some dancing lessons when she was a child."

"Do you still take dance classes a lot?"

Raymie nodded. "Right now, I'm taking an advanced Hip

Hop dance class. It's really fun! But getting back to Marcie, another thing we have in common is that we both care about other people, although she is much more likely to reach out make a new acquaintance than I am. She's quite gregarious."

Raymie stabbed at her salad. "What do I have here, Julie, one of those little round peppers or a cherry tomato? I seem to remember that they sometimes put those peppers in their salads and I don't want to take a bite if it's going to bite back."

Julie, who was used to this kind of question from Raymie, laughed, "It's a tomato. You're safe."

Raymie started to take a bite then stopped and put her fork down. "I think part of what it is about Marcie is that I'm kind of fascinated by her. I've always been intrigued by nuances of communication, hence the profession as a speech therapist, right?" Julie gave Raymie a wry smile that indicated she understood completely. "Marcie wouldn't score very high on an intelligence test, but she's still quite clever."

"How's that?"

"Well, for example, I think she sometimes manipulates a conversation to her advantage by pretending to misunderstand what's been said to her. I've also heard her make statements that might seem rude if anyone else said it, but she has figured out that she can get away with it because of her disability. I don't mean to say that she's malicious or calculating, she just uses what she has to get what she wants, like all of us."

"More power to her," Julie said, giving her coffee a cautious sip.

"She really wanted Shainy and me to come to her house and I tried to put her off by saying we should talk about it again in a couple of weeks and she pretended that she heard me say I'd definitely visit her in two weeks. Now every time I see her, she presses me to choose a day and time to come over."

Julie chuckled. "Pretty clever alright. Are you going to go?"

Raymie looked away, embarrassed by her admission. "Next Saturday."

Julie's laugh was a genuine guffaw. "Raymie, you're such a cream puff! I bet you'll have a great time. Did you say you're taking Shainy?"

"Yes, Marcie enticed me with promises of a play date for Shainy with her dog."

"I bet it'll be fun. This Marcie sounds like a real gem. Are you going to be able to find your way there okay?"

"She gave me the address. She lives on the same street as Kurt, that guy I dated last year, remember?"

"I remember hearing he turned into a real asshole."

"Fortunately, he moved out of town. But anyway, I know the street."

"So, you're all set," Julie said as she licked a bit of mayonnaise off her finger before she took another huge bite of her quickly dwindling sandwich.

Raymie nodded, then said, "I want to tell you about something that happened a couple days ago that illustrates more about Marcie's character."

"Okay," Julie said around her mouthful of food.

"A fellow got on the bus that Marcie had known in high school. Marcie said hi to him and he sat down near us. She asked him about his life and he said he was married and had a son in middle school. Then there was this pregnant pause as we both watched him try to get his shaking under control. The man looked like he had Parkinson's disease. He was shaking quite badly. I politely ignored it, but I think Marcie knew that he wanted to talk about it so she blurted out, 'How come you're so shaky?' The guy actually seemed kind of relieved that she'd asked. I'm sure that most people are too polite to say anything, just like I was. He went on to tell her how tough it's been for him to deal with the disease, and Marcie was very sympathetic."

"So, by being blunt with the guy she gave him the opportunity to talk about how hard it was to have Parkinson's," Julie noted. "Another example of how smart she is?"

"Maybe so. And what's also interesting is that right before the guy got off the bus, he said to Marcie that he was really sorry that he made fun of her in school and Marcie told him that it was a long time ago and no big deal."

"I was really impressed by that. I mean, someone else might have felt vindicated by the guy's illness, saying that he deserved to have a debilitating disease because of how he treated her. Not Marcie, though. Not only did she let bygones be bygones, but she really cared about what the guy was going through."

"That's pretty cool, Raymie," Julie said as she picked up crumbs with a fingertip. "And you realize, of course, that you would have done just the same."

"I don't know about that, Julie. I can be a real witch sometimes."

"Oh," she said, raising an eyebrow, "so you're human?" She leaned forward. "Raymie, you always try to see the other person's point of view. And that seems like something you have in common with this Marcie." Julie paused. "You know, it sounds like you and Marcie share a common philosophy, and that's something that goes beyond things like, I don't know, age, religion or level of intelligence. That kind of stuff."

"Ooh, that's very wise!"

"Thank you. Does that mean you're going to pay for my lunch?"

Raymie laughed. "I had already planned to. It's my turn, anyway."

The afternoon sun glinted off mud puddles left over from yesterday's rain as they strolled back to the office, enjoying the attenuated warmth that signaled the first days of fall. Shainy stopped to lap from a puddle and Julie's phone rang. "I gotta take this," she said. "It's my mechanic."

Half listening to Julie's side of a conversation about her carburetor, Raymie's mind drifted back to Marcie. She was such a strong person, so self-assured. Marcie had told Raymie that it was her older sister, Lisa, the one that died, who taught her to stand up for herself. "You're just as good as anyone else," the sister liked to say. "Don't let anyone tell you different. And if they don't listen to you, you send them to me. I'll make them listen."

What would it be like, Raymie wondered, to have a person like that in her life? If someone had told her that she was just as good as everyone else and encouraged her to speak up for herself would she still be so hesitant to give her opinions, so plagued by uncertainty?

3

Port Angeles, Washington, 1963

Amy Jamison looked over the top of her Life magazine at her daughter who was stretched out on the floor with her coloring book and crayons. "Raymie, you need to adjust your dress. It's riding up." Her eyes returned to her magazine and then she set it aside. "Actually, you should sit up. Young ladies shouldn't lounge around on the floor like that. After all, you're nearly eight years old. Your father thinks that you should start being more ladylike."

"But Mom—"

"No buts, Raymie, this is our decision. The daughter of a minister needs to set a good example for the other little girls in the congregation."

Raymie rolled herself up to a sitting position, then carefully pulled her dress modestly down to cover her thighs. A blue and green plaid with a white Peter Pan collar, the dress was a favorite of hers, but still she wished she could wear pants more often like the other girls. Ducking her head, she said softly, "Mom, will you color with me?"

"If you bring your coloring book and crayons over to the table I can."

"Can't you come and sit on the floor with me?"

Her mother sighed. "I'm sorry sweetheart, I'm just not

feeling very well right now."

"Because of the babies in your tummy?"

"The babies?"

Raymie felt her stomach tense at her mother's tone. "Shelly's mom said that you were going to have twin babies."

"Shelly's mom should mind her own business," her mom said huffily, then: "Oh, Raymie, please forget I said that, that wasn't very nice of me." Amy got up, helped Raymie pick up her crayons so that they could color together at the table. Amy leafed listlessly through the coloring book. "What Shelly's mother said is true, honey. God is bringing a special gift to this home. You are going to have two new brothers or sisters!"

Raymie smiled because her mother was smiling, but she didn't understand. She pushed through her fear of asking the wrong question and said, "Does that mean you're pregnant, like Debbie Ann?"

Raymie saw her mother draw herself up. She frowned, her voice full of disapproval. "Well, yes, I'm pregnant, but a better word to use is *expecting*."

Raymie repeated the word silently to herself, *expecting, expecting*.

Her mother said, "Debbie Ann, honey, that's a different story. You must have overheard me talking to your aunt, so you know that Debbie, well, your cousin Debbie Ann is in trouble, dear, because she's not married. That's a very different thing, and not something we should be talking about. Do you understand?"

Raymie nodded, but really, she didn't understand, except to know that this was one more thing that she had to remember, one more rule to be followed and not questioned. She thought about Debbie Ann, who taught her how to play baseball. She remembered how Debbie had put her baseball cap backwards on Raymie's head and showed her how to hold the bat. "Go get 'em, slugger!" she said, and Raymie had laughed, feeling for once completely accepted and at ease.

Then Raymie's mind turned to the image of the day when there was a new baby at church. The women all crowded around and made cooing noises, asking to hold him and saying things like, "How cute! Look at those little hands. So perfect!" But they weren't going to crowd around Debbie Ann's baby because Debbie was bad: she wasn't married. Raymie ran her fingers through her bangs, thinking if having a baby was a good thing, shouldn't it always be a good thing? What was the big deal about being married? It just wasn't fair.

"Raymie? You're being awfully quiet," her mom said. "Aren't you happy about the new babies coming into our family? You're going to be a big sister!"

Raymie looked up at her mother who seemed to be expecting an enthusiastic response. "Sure, Mom, that will be fun!"

When her mother smiled and patted her on the head Raymie felt the relief of having said the right thing.

4

"Raymie dear."

Raymie's fingers tightened on her book. The words, "Raymie dear" used to signal that something fun was going to happen, like an outing or a game. But not anymore. She looked up to see her mother standing in the open doorway with six-month-old Kevin dangling from her hip, her shirt lopsided where Kevin's hand clutched it. She was still wearing her bedroom slippers and her hair was limp and messy. Where had her pretty mother gone? "I need you to watch Kevin for a while, dear. Keith has messed his diapers something awful and I need to get him into a bath."

Raymie sighed inwardly. She knew better than to let her mom know how reluctant she was to help. "Sure, Mom," she said softly. She put a bookmark in her book and slid off the edge of her bed to reach for the squirming Kevin, whose hands, she noticed, were still sticky from whatever her mom had fed the twins for breakfast. She rubbed her cheek against the fuzz on the top of his head. She loved her brothers, she really did, it was just that she and her mom never did anything special together anymore. Even her eighth birthday party, which was supposed to be so fun, ended up being a disappointment. The twins were just a month old then and her mom was way too busy with them to create her usual magic. Raymie frowned.

So much had changed since the twins were born. Raymie's dancing lessons used to be the highlight of their week and her mom always stayed to watch Raymie practice. Raymie's teacher told her mom that Raymie was a really good dancer – a prodigy, she said – and whatever that meant it made Raymie's mother very proud.

Gently removing Kevin's sticky hand from where he grabbed the frame of her little pink glasses, she put him down on the floor and sat down next to him, handing him her stuffed dog to play with. But mom couldn't stay and watch her dance anymore. The twins were too noisy and active when she took them to the studio, so she now would just drop Raymie off and pick her up afterward.

Kevin had started to gnaw on the dog's paw, making his funny little humming noise. Raymie smiled slightly, leaning over to straighten the collar of his little blue shirt. Then she sighed. It was Saturday. She'd done her morning chores and was just starting to get into her book. No hope for that now. She'd have to watch Kevin at least until her mom finished bathing Keith and then it would be nearly time for lunch when her mom would probably want Raymie to help feed one of the boys.

Kevin looked up at her and Raymie grinned and gave him a little tickle under the chin and he laughed, making her laugh back at him. You weren't supposed to have favorites, but still, she might like Kevin best, at least most of the time. But sometimes she thought she might like Keith best, because he had his own way to charm her. The twins weren't identical, but they were both so cute, and looked enough alike that her mom dressed them in matching outfits. People would stop and smile at them whenever they took them on an outing.

Kevin had let go of the stuffed dog and started crawling toward her box of paper dolls. She grabbed him around the waist and reached over to take her sock monkey off the end of her bed and handed it to him, hoping he wouldn't get to much drool on it. She wished her mom would hurry up.

Raymie wanted to be able to enjoy her Saturday because tomorrow was Sunday and Sundays seemed so long and boring. When she was littler, she looked forward to Sundays. Her dad held two services each Sunday, and Raymie got to be in Sunday school during both of them, which was pretty fun, but now that she was bigger she had to attend one of the services, where she would have to listen to the sermon that she'd already heard several times at home. Her dad liked to practice aloud with her mom as an audience.

Going to church used to be such a special time for her. She remembered how good it felt when the women at church would exclaim over her pretty dresses and strawberry blonde curls. "So pretty, so dainty! And I hear that you've started her in dance classes," they'd say to her mother. "You must be so proud of her!" Back then Raymie felt like she was important to her mom and dad. She even had a special name that came from both of her parents. "Raymie is a blend of Ray and Amy," her mother would explain to the attentive listener while beaming at Raymie and giving the little hand she was holding a squeeze, and as she looked up at her mother and heard the oft-told story about her name, Raymie would know how completely she *belonged.*

Now, with everyone cooing over her brothers, she was no longer at center stage and Raymie often felt like the extra child, a dispensable member of the family. Because of that she tried even harder to be good, watching her parents closely for signs of how she should act and feel. And there was no lack of information about that. They always saw something she was doing wrong, something that needed correction.

Now it seemed like her brothers were the special ones, everybody's favorites. There were days when she hated her brothers, Raymie thought, eying Kevin with annoyance. Then immediately regretting that thought she scooped the surprised Kevin up into her arms, hugging him to her so hard that he gave a little frightened squeak. "Sorry Kevin," she muttered as she let him go. Smoothing his hair, she wondered with exasperation, couldn't she do anything right?

"Are you ready to go, Raymie?"

Raymie finished buckling her shoe before straightening up to call into the next room. "Yes, Mom, I'll be right there."

It was the next day, Sunday, and Raymie was wearing a new dress. Well, new to her; it had belonged to Melanie, her cousin in California. She and Melanie were close in age, but because Raymie was smaller than most of the other girls, Melanie's hand-me-downs fit her perfectly. Raymie ran her hand over the soft fabric. The dress was one of her favorite colors, a soft turquoise blue, and her mom said it was an A-line, which was a style that the older girls were wearing. Raymie's mom didn't approve of it. She could tell by how Amy pursed her lips when Raymie tried it on; it wasn't like the babyish full-skirted dresses that her mom picked out for her, but Raymie loved it and wearing it almost made up for having to be at church for most of that day.

She walked into the kitchen where her parents were waiting for her, each holding a twin.

"Isn't that dress a little mature for her?" Raymie's dad said, while adjusting his grip on Keith.

"Oh, well, but she really likes it, Ray."

"Humph. I guess since she already has it on."

Raymie let out the long breath that she hadn't known she was holding. Sometimes her dad would make her change out of what she'd chosen to wear, like when she put on her blue jeans to go to the pumpkin carving party and he made her go back to her room and put on a dress. "Girls don't go to parties dressed in pants!" he almost shouted at her. He was wrong, and Raymie was embarrassed to be the only one there in a dress.

When they got to the church, Mrs. Alcore, who had a key, was already there, busily setting up the food for the after-church social. Raymie felt disappointed when she saw Mrs. Alcore's big arms hovering over the plate of cookies, her solid legs planted like trees in front of the counter. Usually the cookies were Raymie's job. She loved to line them up in rows, dark against light, and sometimes there was even a broken one she would be allowed to eat.

"Thanks, Jenny," Amy said to Mrs. Alcore as she deposited the twins in the play pen in a corner of the large kitchen. "You can go ahead and let Raymie finish the cookies. I brought the lunchmeat if you don't mind helping with the finger sandwiches."

Raymie smiled gratefully at her mother as she pulled out the red metal step stool, just the right size for her to comfortably reach the counter.

As the women moved to the other end of the kitchen to confer about the finger sandwiches, Raymie heard a "psst" and looked over her shoulder to see Mrs. Alcore's middle daughter Denise standing at her elbow. Raymie was surprised to see her. On the Sundays when their mom came in early to help in the church kitchen the Alcore kids usually came later with their dad, right before the service started.

"Those cookies sure look good," Denise said, placing a foot on the bottom step of the two-tiered step stool. She lowered her voice. "You ever drop any of them?"

"Oh no, I'm very careful!"

"If you dropped some and they landed, say, in my purse"—she opened her little plastic purse, something which Raymie's mom had declared a frivolity for a girl her age—"then there might be an invitation to my birthday party next week."

Raymie looked at the open purse, then at Denise. They were in the same class at school, but Denise usually ignored Raymie in favor of the more popular girls. Raymie didn't care that much if Denise and her friends played with her or not, but because they had such superior attitudes, she reasoned that she probably should care.

She dropped two cookies into Denise's purse.

"Two cookies? Is that all?"

Raymie looked over to where her mother was occupied with Mrs. Alcore. She dropped in two more.

Denise looked at the cookies and rolled her eyes.

"If I give you too many more they're going to notice," Raymie whispered.

"No, they won't!" Denise declared, the level of her voice rising enough to draw attention.

"What's going on over there?" Mrs. Alcore began moving very quickly over to the two girls. She saw Denise clutching her purse and snatched it out of her hands. "What's this?" she said angrily. She gave Denise a little slap across the back of her head. "At it again, are you?"

"She talked me into it!" Denise declared righteously, pointing a finger at Raymie.

By then Raymie's mother had joined them, a look of horror on her face.

Mrs. Alcore glanced at her. "No big deal, Amy, just girls and their hijinks." She looked at Denise. "Put them back and there'll be no more said about it. Then go on outside and see if your dad is here yet. This is the last time you get to come in early with me."

Denise reached into her purse and set the cookies onto the plate. As she watched, Raymie felt a shadow behind her and turned to see her father standing in the kitchen doorway in his robe. Mrs. Burke, who played the organ, and a couple of early arriving church members were crowding in behind him. "What's going on here?" he asked sternly.

Raymie's mom looked at her husband, her eyes pleading with him to let it go.

"We'll talk about this later," he said, straightening the robe over the sleeve of the white shirt underneath. "Raymie, get down from there and help your mother get the twins into the nursery room. The service starts in fifteen minutes. No Sunday School for you today."

After getting the details of what had happened Amy had tried her best to arbitrate for her daughter, but Ray Jamieson was furious. "God commands us not to steal, Raymie, you know that," her father told her that evening as he prepared to spank her. "What you have done is a transgression against God."

Raymie looked at the overly clean hands that so rudely pulled her dress up, the dress she had been so proud of, to expose her bottom for the spanking. Those hands that were always so gentle and soft when he stood at the pulpit were now strong and unforgiving as contact was made with her skin. How could they be the same pair of hands? She remembered those hands swinging her in circles while they both laughed. Now they always seemed to be clenched in anger.

Afterward he made Raymie sit on the couch, telling her to think about what she had done. "Your father works hard to teach his congregation to follow the word of God," her mother explained gently. "What you did showed a lack of respect for your father and his position in this community." Her father, standing in front of Raymie with his arms crossed, added, "You might have thought you were just having a little fun with your friend, but you have brought shame to us in front of the whole congregation."

Raymie put her head down and curved in her shoulders, wishing she could make her body small enough to disappear. She felt a part of herself shrinking away from her parents, especially her father. She accepted her isolation on the couch as part of her punishment, but when she was released and allowed to join the family again a part of her remained aloof and watchful. The feeling of separateness from them came over her like a heavy blanket and she huddled beneath it, quiet and alone.

Over the next few years, the invisible act of pulling away from her parents bled into Raymie's relationship with their church. She was wary of what she was being taught in Sunday school, puzzled by the fact that it didn't always make sense to her but aware that she would be expected to swallow her uncertainty. When she was eleven and in a Sunday school class taught by a particularly rigid member of the congregation, her confusion over the words of the second commandment overcame her reticence to challenge what she was being taught, and she ventured, "What does it mean that God is a jealous god? Isn't jealousy supposed to be a bad thing?"

Her teacher's face, previously a mask of kindness, hardened, and the other kids turned to look at Raymie. "God's jealousy is a different kind of jealousy. You'll understand that better when you grow up. You just have to believe," the teacher explained condescendingly, "like God expects you to, like a little child, without question."

Suddenly the frustration from all the times Raymie had been shut down when she wanted to speak rose to the surface. "Oh, you mean I should believe in God like how a little kid believes in the tooth fairy? I don't get it. Why did God give us brains if he didn't want us to think about things and ask questions? That's just stupid!" Raymie heard herself thump her bible closed in exasperation, knowing even as she did that she had gone too far.

The content of this conversation was relayed to her father as soon as Raymie's Sunday school teacher found a moment to draw him aside. That evening her father sat down with Raymie and explained at length what the second commandment meant, droning on just like he did in his sermons. She nodded and thanked him as was expected of her, but it still didn't feel right to Raymie. She knew that she was being willful, and privately, she didn't care. Why shouldn't she have questions? If God was supposed to be such a loving god, why would he not love the part of her that questioned?

5

As Raymie entered adolescence she became aware of some interesting changes in her mother. It was now the late nineteen-sixties and the country was in the throes of the cultural revolution. Women were examining their lives and pursuing interests beyond home and family, and Raymie's mother was no exception. When an old friend from college contacted Amy to ask her if she would take a part time job at the bookstore she was opening, Amy didn't hesitate before saying yes.

The argument between Raymie's parents about the job at the bookstore was cut short by Amy's insistence that she could still fulfill her duties as the wife of a minister and mother to her three children. "I've always been a good helpmate to you, Ray, you have to admit that, and I can't see why that would change. I can still organize activities at church, and now that the twins are in school there is no reason why I can't take this job. Eileen says she really needs me. You probably remember that we used to work in the university bookstore together." She looked at Raymie's father, who gave her a guarded nod. "And it might only be until she and her husband get the store up and running."

It was subtle at first, the difference in her mother. First it was just her mood. She seemed happier after she started the job and sometimes sang to herself while she was doing chores around the house, songs Raymie had never heard her sing before. Then slowly the clothing she wore to work changed from her usual demure dress or slacks to jeans and brightly colored tops.

Knowing that Raymie liked to read as much as she did, Amy started bringing home books for her, offering to discuss plot and character. Raymie loved these discussions, feeling close to her mom for the first time since before the twins were born.

Working at the bookstore opened Amy up to new ideas, as well as some she'd abandoned to mold herself more completely to her husband's vision of the world. She had been an English literature major when she met and married Ray, and dropped out of college in order to help him establish the church. Now back in the world of books, she discovered ideas that she had previously discarded and people who were willing to discuss those ideas with her. She was invited to join a book club through the store and found that gave her much more satisfaction than the ladies' bible study group that she led at church. Although Amy continued to fulfill her duties as minister's wife her enthusiasm was forced, her attention elsewhere. She started to delegate her duties at the church to other women, and eventually even had someone else take over the bible study group, explaining to Ray that it would free up time for her to tend to the needs of their children. Raymie knew that her mom just simply didn't want to lead the group anymore and thought her dad knew it too, though he just frowned when Amy told him.

As her mother pulled away from the church Raymie watched, both puzzled and intrigued by the process. She saw that Amy was forming friendships outside of the congregation, women who probably didn't even go to church, and Raymie wondered if her mother still shared her father's faith.

It was shortly after her fifteenth birthday when Raymie

asked her mother about this. She was sitting at the table doing homework and could hear the twins' exuberant voices outside the window as they played with their friends in the backyard. Her mom was reading a book, "The Feminine Mystique," for her book club. Raymie noticed that Amy tucked the book away whenever her dad was around.

"Mom," she said, setting down her pencil, "do you still believe in God? It seems like you're sort of questioning that, just like I am."

Her mom looked at her, surprised.

"It's not like I want to say anything about it to Dad," Raymie explained, a blush coming to her cheeks. "I just wanted to know for myself."

"Well," Amy said, laying her bookmark inside a page, "my idea about what God is seems to have evolved a bit over time so that I'm not sure exactly what I believe anymore." She made a little grimace. "But you know, we need to think about your dad. Even if he and I might have different ideas, the church is his livelihood and it's important for us to support him."

"I just don't think I believe in God, at least not the way Dad does. The God he talks about sounds mean, condemning people to a lake of fire and all that. That's horrible! I don't think I could do that to anyone, no matter how bad they'd been. What happened to, 'do unto others'?"

Amy gave a soft chuckle. "I can tell that you've really been thinking about this." Then, with a little frown, she added, "And, honey, it's alright to have your own beliefs, but for your dad's sake I need you to act as though you believe just as he does."

"Okay," Raymie sighed. She was used to pretending, to holding back and guarding the most essential, the most tender, parts of herself.

Amy smiled at her daughter softly, tilted her head in an apology of sorts before picking up her book to resume reading.

Raymie looked at her mother's bent head, the slightly crooked part in the dark hair, a lock tucked behind one ear. A sudden love for her came over Raymie, stronger than the day to day love she always felt, as she saw Amy not just as her mom, but as a whole person, a person apart from the roles she had always filled in their family.

This shift in perception was followed by a moment of disorientation, and Raymie sensed an edge of vulnerability creep in. She liked the changes in her mother, even felt a little amused by them, noticing her mom was a bit like a teenager herself, still finding out who she really was. Raymie was glad that her mother was also questioning her beliefs; it helped her feel not so alone. But there was also this touch of nausea, a roll in the pit of her stomach. Her world, once so stable, was becoming an altered place. If her mom, who represented what was steady and reliable in her life, could change, what could she rely on to stay the same?

Outside the window they heard a squabble rise between the twins, something about a toy that each claimed as his own. Amy gave a little sigh as she put down her book and stood to go and intervene in the argument, and by so doing, restored the equilibrium that Raymie had momentarily lost. In the end, Amy was, after all, still essentially the person she had always known as her mom, and always would be.

6

SEVERAL MONTHS LATER Raymie was at Lucinda Davidson's dance studio dressing for class, hands smoothing her tights over her legs before slipping on her dance shoes. The benches in the dressing room were cold on this late winter day and Raymie had shivered as she changed out of her school clothes, but she didn't mind. She would be happy to dance under any conditions.

She looked around her. The studio dressing room was small and makeshift and unless she came in early like today, she'd be jostled by the other girls while changing, but this slightly shabby downtown space felt like home. The minute she came through the heavy double doors of the studio, everything – her parents, the church, the pressure at school – would all fall away and with the first few dance steps she would feel herself become whole again.

Raymie couldn't remember a time when she didn't love to dance; her earliest memories were of the joy of movement. She had a natural ability to mimic dance steps and to know instinctively how her body moved through space: the swoops, steps and leaps that make up a dance, the exhilarating rush of air as she twirled. Delighted by her daughter's ability, Raymie's mother enrolled her in dance classes when she was only four years old. Raymie learned ballet with a group of mostly older girls, doing plies and arabesques to the scratchy classical music and children's songs played on an old phonograph in Lucinda's first studio, a converted garage a few blocks away from Raymie's house.

Raymie closed her locker and pushed aside the curtain that separated the dressing room from the practice room.

"First one here again?" Lucinda said, smiling indulgently at Raymie, her best and favorite student.

"Yes, I thought I'd spend a few minutes practicing before the others get here," Raymie said just as her friend Helene burst into the door, quickly followed by a second student. Raymie waved as the girls hurried into the dressing room.

She turned back to Lucinda, who asked, "You're a sophomore in high school this year, is that right?"

Raymie nodded, curious about why Lucinda was asking.

"So, you'll be sixteen soon?"

"In May."

"Okay. The reason I'm asking is because I've leased the empty building next to this one so I can expand the school. Would you be interested in doing some teaching this summer? I need someone for the grade school students."

"Oh, yes! I'd love to do that!"

"Wonderful! I'll keep that in mind," Lucinda said as another student came through the door, bringing the cool air in with her. "Right now, I have to get ready for class, but there'll be plenty of time to talk more before the new space is complete."

Raymie watched her walk away, wondering if the job offer was Lucinda's way of making up for the conversation they'd had a couple of weeks ago. Asking her to sit down with her for a talk, Lucinda had told Raymie what she already suspected: unless the short, compact physique inherited from her father magically changed into a tall willowy form, she just didn't have the body type that was sought in a ballerina, making Raymie's chance of someday being selected for a ballet troupe slim, no matter how good she was. Raymie was taking two ballet classes a week and one in jazz, Lucinda noted; perhaps she'd like to concentrate more heavily on jazz? Raymie cried when Lucinda said this, and her teacher, who had started to cry too, reached out to give her an awkward hug.

Since then Raymie had moved her focus to jazz, giving it the same dedication that she had formerly given ballet. It helped that jazz was fun and the environment in the class was looser and felt less competitive than that of her ballet class. She'd even found a new friend there.

Her friend Helene, a tall, slender girl with a prominent nose and thick-lashed eyes, was almost a year older than Raymie and attended school in the neighboring district. She had a deep, warm laugh, and had a huge repertoire of swear words at her command, which she muttered under her breath over anything that displeased her, causing Raymie to laugh out loud in admiration. Raymie liked Helene's easy-going disposition and her ability to laugh at her own mistakes. She encouraged Raymie, who was very self-critical, to do the same and Raymie adored her for it.

After they'd known each other for a few months Helene invited Raymie to come and practice their routines at her house. Raymie asked her parents and because Helene came from what her father considered a good home, Raymie was allowed to spend time with her. There was a full basement in Helene's family home, sparsely furnished, where she and Raymie could practice. They made up their own dance routines and day-dreamed about being famous dancers with admiring fans.

"Before we meet fame and fortune, we have to go to a prestigious performing arts school. I've decided I'm going to train at Juilliard in New York," Helene declared with a fanciful sweep of her arm.

"Oh, that sounds wonderful! But isn't it extremely expensive?"

"No problem. My folks have beaucoup bucks. I can go anywhere I want."

"I would love to be able to go to Cornish in Seattle," Raymie said wistfully. "That's where Lucinda went."

"*Seattle?* No way! Reach for the stars, girl! You're coming to New York with me. You have great talent!"

Raymie laughed and gave Helene a deep ballet curtsey, brushing back an imaginary tutu that she knew was about as real as the possibility of studying in New York.

Life got busy for Raymie and Helene. Raymie started her job teaching ballet to the younger kids and Helene was hired to teach jazz on days alternating with the class Raymie taught. Helene now had a steady boyfriend and on the rare occasions she and Raymie got together the main topic of her conversation was Gary.

"It sounds like you and Gary are pretty serious about each other," Raymie commented after the third time in a matter of minutes Helene had made reference to something Gary said or did.

"I'd say so!" Helene told her. "He's the guy I'm going to marry."

"Whoa! I mean, are you sure? You're only sixteen."

"Seventeen in less than a month, actually. Gary and I are talking about getting married when I'm eighteen. We both want lots of kids and don't see any reason why not to get started right away."

"But what about New York? I thought you wanted to get a degree in performing arts?"

Helene shrugged. "Yeah, maybe," then reacting to the disappointment on Raymie's face, said: "Maybe I'll go to school first, then have my kids after that, you never know. But Gary's a great guy and we want the same things out of life. Not everybody gets that. People spend a whole lifetime looking for the right person. I'm not going to pass this up."

"I suppose not," Raymie told her, believing that Helene would eventually give up the idea. "Well, but you still want to dance no matter what, right?"

Helene gave a little snort of laughter. "Absolutely! This is me you're talking to, your friend Helene! Duh! Now what about that routine you wanted to show me?"

7

OTHER THAN THE one class a week that they had together with Lucinda, Raymie saw very little of Helene over the next year. Where once they might have spent time together after class, Helene would leave right after with Gary, who came to pick her up.

When Helene gave her an invitation to her eighteenth birthday party, Raymie said she would go and invited her current boyfriend, who ended up having to work that night. Disappointed, Raymie borrowed her mother's car and drove herself to the apartment where Gary, who was three years older than Helene, lived with a couple of other guys. Raymie held onto the metal rail as she walked up to the upper row of apartments in the run-down building, taking the stairs carefully in the dim light. Her night vision wasn't very good; the eye doctor thought contact lenses would help, but Raymie didn't really see a difference. She found the apartment, and standing alone at the door and listening to the loud voices behind it, she almost turned to go.

Raymie was still undecided when the door was opened by Gary. "Come on in, Raymie," he said affably. "Let me get you a beer."

Raymie looked around her as she walked through the door. The apartment was small and stuffy and thronged with people

Raymie didn't know. It was made even stuffier by the smell of cigarette smoke, frozen pizza cooking in the oven and spilled beer. "Thanks," she told Gary, "but I had better have a soda or something. I don't want to go home smelling like alcohol."

Gary handed her a can of coke. "Drink some of that down," he said, and after she had a couple of gulps, he snagged a bottle off the crowded drinks table and filled her can to the top. "Now if your folks smell alcohol you can tell them that someone must have spiked your drink." He grinned. "Just don't say it was me!"

Raymie smiled and tasted her coke. Whatever Gary had added to it, it was quite alcoholic. She'd have to watch it. Her parents had made her promise she wouldn't drink.

"Hey! There she is!" Raymie heard Helene say in a voice that already sounded a little slurred. "Welcome to Gary's humble abode. Did you get something to drink?"

Raymie raised her soda can in answer, then said, "How are you, Helene? Are you having a good birthday so far?"

"The best ever, Raymie. Look what Gary gave me this morning!" She held out her hand so that Raymie could admire her ring. "Gary and I are getting married right after graduation. I'd love for you to come to the wedding."

"Married?" Raymie said stupidly.

"Yes, Raymie, like I told you before, Gary and I are getting married. You know, as in husband and wife." Helene said, an edge of irritation in her voice. "People do it all the time. And the usual response to this kind of announcement is, 'Congratulations!' or 'I know you'll be very happy together.'"

"Oh! Yes, of course! Congratulations, Helene." Raymie frowned, the confusion apparent on her face. "So, are you still planning to go to a performing arts school?'"

"Naw. Gary's been working for my dad for the past couple

of years and now that Dad is opening a new branch in Olympia, he's going to train Gary in management. Isn't that cool? We'll be moving there right after we get married."

"Oh. That sounds wonderful, Helene. But what about dancing?"

"Hey, yeah! I'm not giving that up! We're gonna be looking for a house with some kind of a space that can be made into a studio. I plan to give lessons to little kids. I've been talking to Lucinda and she told me how she started up her school by teaching ballet in the garage she fixed up."

"You talked to Lucinda about this?"

"Uh huh." Helene took a long drink of her beer, then turned when another girl tapped her on the shoulder and handed her a joint.

"And she didn't say you should dance professionally? You're awfully good, Helene."

"Yeah, that's true," Helene said as she took a quick hit. "But Lucinda knows me. She knows my dreams for a home and family and she thinks teaching is a good idea."

Raymie was silent, stunned to realize how much Helene's hopes for the future differed from her own.

"You look surprised, Raymie." Helene narrowed her eyes and tipped her head to one side. "You know, maybe you should talk to Lucinda yourself. She's pretty good at helping her students figure out the next step."

"But I know the next step. I'm going to be a professional dancer."

"Are you?" Helene said.

Someone hollered out from the kitchen that the pizza was done and Helene gave Raymie a little hug before she said, "I gotta take care of the pizza. Let's talk later."

Helene's words had felt like an affront. Where did she get off acting so superior? The words stung all the more because Raymie was beginning to have her own doubts about a career in dance. Her parents were dead set against it, her father saying that he wouldn't pay for a performing arts school, that Raymie had to go to a regular university and major in something he deemed practical.

Despite her annoyance with Helene, Raymie agreed that it probably would be a good idea to talk to Lucinda. The opportunity came two days later after class. Raymie waited until the other students had left, lingering in the dressing room until she heard Lucinda start to clean up in preparation to close for the day.

She walked over to where Lucinda was sweeping. "Lucinda, I need to talk to you about something. Do you have a moment?"

Lucinda turned to see Raymie standing behind her. "Oh hello, Raymie. I hadn't realized that you were still here." She leaned the broom against the wall. "I'd be happy to talk with you." She indicated the two metal folding chairs in the corner of the room and they went to sit down.

Lucinda was silent, her face kind, as she waited for Raymie to speak.

Raymie hesitated before plunging ahead. "I really need to know your opinion of my future as a professional dancer."

"Well," Lucinda said, brushing a spot on her leotard evasively, "you're certainly quite talented and you have the kind of dedication needed to be successful in that kind of work."

"But I'm short," Raymie broke in.

Lucinda sighed, perhaps a little vexed with Raymie for being so blunt. "Your diminutive stature could be a problem. If you continue to work very hard, you could overcome that, but it wouldn't be easy."

Raymie slumped forward on the metal chair, her elbows on her knees and her chin in her hands. "Let's face it, I'm barely over five feet. I looked ridiculous when I tried partner dancing and I stick out like a sore thumb in a dance line. I'm not stupid, Lucinda. I know that I've got a problem here."

"Now, don't get me wrong, Raymie. You could do it. You could be a professional dancer. But the going would be tough. You'd have to work very hard to prove yourself. Add to that the long hours and always being on the move." She leaned back in her chair. "I'm sure you've heard me talk about the years that I was with a dance company. It didn't take me long to realize that it wasn't as glamorous as it seemed from the outside." She leaned forward again so she could catch Raymie's eye. "I'm just thinking that may not be the life you want."

Raymie wiped the tear that had started to roll down her cheek and sat up in her chair. "You're right, Lucinda. That probably really isn't the life I want."

They were both silent a few moments before Lucinda asked, "Is there anything else you'd like to do?"

Taking a deep breath, Raymie said slowly, "Well, there is one thing. A few years ago, my brother Keith was referred to a speech therapist. I went with Mom so I could watch my other brother while Mom went into the appointment with Keith. I got to learn a little bit about what the speech therapist did and I was really fascinated by her work, you know?" She looked at Lucinda who smiled in encouragement. "I've been thinking lately that if I don't go in to dance, I might like to do that."

"That sounds like very interesting work!" Lucinda told her, earnestly excited for Raymie. "And you know of course, choosing not to dance professionally doesn't mean you have to stop dancing altogether."

"Just try to stop me," Raymie said, choking on a laugh and angerly wiping another tear. "I would dance deaf, dumb and blind."

"I do believe you would." Lucinda told her, the shine of pride in her eyes. "You're made of good stuff, Raymie; anyone can see that."

As she let the warmth of Lucinda's praise flow through her, a shift occurred within Raymie. She wasn't going to be a great dancer after all, and that was okay. She was going to be someone who helped other people improve their lives. She tried that on and it felt very solid and good.

Raymie rose from her chair and Lucinda got up to stand with her. "I guess I'll go tell my parents what I've decided," she told Lucinda. "I just hope they don't say I told you so."

"Oh, I imagine they'll have the wisdom to resist that," Lucinda said with a teasing smile.

8

Poulsbo, Washington, September 2013

Raymie was a few months shy of her forty-ninth birthday when she received the diagnosis. "You will eventually be blind. Not blind-blind," the retina specialist explained, putting his hands over his eyes, "but this disorder is degenerative, which means it's likely that you will be legally blind within the next decade, if not sooner."

Raymie had suspected that something was very wrong with her vision, but it still was a shock to hear the prognosis. She grieved, the loss weighing her down for days, then pulled herself up, resolving to do what she could to preserve her sight. She used the eye drops the retinologist prescribed, took herbs to increase eye health, tried massage and acupuncture and exercises designed to increase clarity. Still the darkness crept in, colors faded, objects became blurry. It came by degrees, giving her time to get used to it, like slowly wading into frigid water.

The year that she met Marcie Raymie's blindness wasn't very advanced as of yet. Still able to experience quite a bit of independence, she decided against asking a friend for a ride to Marcie's house. As she had told her co-worker Julie, she knew the street from when a former boyfriend lived there, and the bus driver was very happy to help her get off at the right stop.

It was the last week of September, but the fair weather had

held, so the day was sunny and not terribly cold. She and Shainy had a pleasant walk through the nicely maintained neighborhood, the older homes on either side of the street bracketed by well-grown trees and tall hedges.

Marcie had described the house to Raymie, a white two-story toward the end of the block, and they'd agreed that she would call Marcie when she got close.

"Marcie," Raymie spoke into her phone and as it dialed the number, Raymie thought again about how quickly this quirky woman had found her way into her life. When Marcie answered, Raymie said, "Hi Marcie, it's me, Raymie. I think I'm almost at your house."

"Yay!" Marcie said, and Raymie felt a flush of pleasure at her exuberance. "I can see you down the street! Keep walking and I'll wave to you when you get closer."

A few moments later Raymie heard her call out, "Rainy!" and had a moment of confusion before she remembered that Rainy was Marcie's nickname for her. Raymie looked ahead and saw a moving shape at the front of a house. Shainy gave a little whine of recognition and as Raymie moved closer the shape became Marcie waving at her in wide arcs. Marcie walked over to open the gate of the little fence that surrounded the front lawn and Raymie followed her up the front steps. There was the sound of a dog barking behind the door and she sensed Shainy tensing with the anticipation of meeting another dog. She was still young and loved to play.

"Welcome to our house!" Marcie said, then she opened the door a crack to keep her dog, who was still barking, from rushing out. "Shh, Shep, she's okay, these are friends!" she told the dog, then opened the door fully and a big fluffy dog came bounding out toward Raymie, his huge tail displacing air as he waved it in welcome. Standing just inside the door, Raymie and Marcie introduced the dogs to one another, and even though Shainy stayed by Raymie's side as she was trained to do, the answering wag of her tail indicated that the dogs would be great friends in no time.

"Want me to hang up your coat?" Marcie asked.

Nodding, Raymie shrugged out of her coat, letting Marcie put it on a coat rack that was humped several layers deep with coats. "Come on into the kitchen," she said. "That's where we hang out the most." She led Raymie through the living room and down the hall.

"Hey Marcie, was that your friend at the door?" a masculine voice called out. "I'm looking for another cold soda for your friend but I only see one in here."

As they walked into a brightly lit kitchen, Raymie saw what looked to her like a youngish man dressed in jeans and a dark shirt with the tails untucked, bent over the open refrigerator, one hand holding the door open while he rummaged around with the other. "Oh, never mind, here's another one!" He turned in triumph, sodas in hand, and bumped his head on the edge of the open fridge. "Ow!" he said, rubbing a spot on the top of his head with the heel of his hand. Raymie smiled in pained sympathy, and felt an instant liking for the tall, lanky man standing before her. He was much older than her original estimation; she could make out that his hair was a nice whitish-gray and that he had deep lines on either side of his mouth.

He stopped in mid-motion, the refrigerator door still open, apparently needing to recover himself before turning to close the door. When he turned back, he seemed surprised by Raymie.

Raymie smiled to herself. Marcie had probably described

her as her blind friend or something in that order, but Raymie wasn't wearing dark glasses or carrying her cane, the only tip-off being Shainy in her guide dog harness. Raymie knew that her small stature may also have puzzled him. She wasn't just short; she was also slender and small-boned. Even now, when she was in her late fifties, at first glance she might be mistaken for a child.

Raymie was equally perplexed by Jack. If this was Marcie's brother, as she suspected, they must have had different fathers or something. Where Marcie was only slightly taller than Raymie, and was chubby and dark complexioned, this man was fair-skinned, tall and slender.

"This is Rainy, Jack," Marcie announced. "And that's Shainy there beside her, being a good girl," she said, stroking Shainy's head. "Unlike other dogs here who will remain not named," she added in mock disapproval as the overly exuberant Shep, his tail swishing like mad, poked his nose into Shainy's face.

Jack set the cokes on the counter, wiped his hands on the back of his jeans, and reached out to shake hands. "Hi Rainy," he said.

"Hello," she said, taking his hand. His handshake was warm and firm and she noticed she didn't want to let go as quickly as would be polite. "And actually," she told him, "my real name is Raymie. Rainy is just what Marcie calls me."

He held onto her hand a moment longer while he seemed to process that. "Oh. Well, nice to meet you, Raymie." Then he tipped his head to one side. "I was going to offer you something. Marcie likes Diet Coke, but there's also coffee or tea. Or a beer?"

Raymie barely stifled a smile of amusement as he opened his hands and shrugged broadly, expressing that he knew adding beer to the list of offerings may have been a little odd.

She wondered if he was feeling the same tension she did. There was no question that she was attracted to this guy.

Raymie turned to Marcie. "What are you going to have?"

"I'm gonna have a soda."

"Well, then, I'll join you."

Jack seemed to relax a little as he put the sodas on the table. "Glass?" he asked.

"Hell no!" Marcie interjected, her voice almost jubilant. "It's better right out of the can." She pulled out a chair to sit at the kitchen table, motioning Raymie to sit down. As she got into her chair, Raymie said, "Thank you Jack, this is perfect."

He inclined his head toward Shainy, who Raymie had released from her leash. "Beautiful dog," he said as Shep approached her with a deep play bow to which Shainy responded with a playful bark and a little sideways jump.

"In the living room with you, you two ruffians," Marcie told the dogs, pointing to the adjacent room, and the dogs trotted off together.

"Well," Jack said, reluctance apparent in his voice, "I'll let you two visit." He started to move out of the room.

"No way, Jack!" Marcie said. "Sit down and talk with us awhile!"

"Oh yes, please do," Raymie told him.

Jack went to the counter where Raymie could hear him pour himself a cup of coffee. The rich aroma was enticing; it was good coffee no doubt, and strong, but she had committed to Diet Coke, which she sipped tentatively.

He pulled out a chair and sat down between them at the table, set his mug down in front of him, then picked it up again to cup it in his hands. Raymie wondered if he felt as uncomfortable as she did.

Marcie, perhaps sensing their discomfort, turned her head toward the living room where they could hear the sound of the two dogs playing. "I knew they'd like each other!" she said.

Jack chuckled. "Shep really needed a friend. He gets a little stir-crazy sometimes without any kids around." He had just started to take another sip of coffee when his shirt pocket began to play a tinny rendition of "Flight of the Valkyries." Jack reached in to pull out his phone, frowning a little as he looked at the screen.

"Oh brother," Marcie said.

Jack ignored her. "You'll have to excuse me. I'm going to have to take this," he said as he rose from the table.

"Yeah, like it's the third time she's called today. I guess you better answer it this time," Marcie muttered. "Don't mind us," she added with just a touch of sarcasm.

Raymie looked at Marcie in surprise. She hadn't seen her be so uncharitable before. Whoever was on the phone, Marcie clearly didn't like her.

Raymie looked at Jack. "No problem," she said to smooth things over, even as she noticed her disappointment that he couldn't spend more time with them. Jack left the room, abandoning his mug of coffee on the table.

Raymie stifled a desire to reach out and touch the mug, maybe take a little sip. She curled her fingers more tightly around her Coke can, unsure if this impulse had to do with wanting to taste his coffee so much as to touch what he had touched, to put her mouth where he had put his.

Startled by this thought, annoyed with herself, she quickly pushed it away. She was here to visit with Marcie. Her interest in the brother just wasn't appropriate.

9

"Well, so that was Jack," Marcie told Raymie after he had left the kitchen. "Too bad, but we probably won't see him again for a while. She talks and talks, boring him outta his gourd I think, though he never says it."

Raymie wanted to ask who Marcie was referring to. Jack's mother? His sister or a girlfriend? The opportunity passed as she tried to decide if it would be impolite or not.

Marcie tipped her head back to take a couple of deep gulps of soda, and changed the subject by emitting a long burp, looking pleased with herself.

Raymie gave a surprised bark of a laugh, and Marcie met her eyes, laughing too. She drank the last dregs of her soda and said, "Let me show you the rest of the house."

"I'd love to see more of your house!' Raymie rose from the table taking the two cans, hers still half-full, to the counter and setting them by the sink. "Do you have recycling?" she asked.

"Under the sink," Marcie replied and Raymie quietly poured out the rest of her soda, then opened the cupboard door under the sink and felt inside the bin there to make sure she was putting the cans in the right place.

"So," Marcie said as Raymie washed her hands at the sink, "you already saw the living room when we came in. This next room over is the dining room that we hardly never use anymore." She moved down the hall. "Here's the downstairs bathroom with my towel on the floor." Raymie peeked into the dimly lit room to see what was maybe a pedestal sink and a clawfoot tub while Marcie picked up the towel and tossed it toward a rack where it sat for a moment before it slid off again. Marcie shrugged and started down the hall again. "Those are the stairs to the bedrooms where the boys used to sleep," she said, motioning to an open stairwell, its wooden stairs steep and narrow. "They're all grown up now but sometimes they visit and then they sleep there." She walked a little further down the hall. "And down here is my room." The dogs had joined them by then and Shep pushed his way into the room, but Shainy waited for a brief nod from Raymie before following. The bedroom Raymie stepped into was large and comfortable. On the wall facing them were three long windows dressed with lacy white curtains.

"What a pretty room!" she exclaimed.

"Thanks, I like it too, and I have everything I need here, like this is my TV and there's my stereo and my records." Marcie went over to her dresser and picked up a small framed photograph. "Here's me with a gold medal for my Special Olympics swimming team, but you really can't see that very well, can you?"

"No, not really, but I'm sure you look very proud."

"I sure do," Marcie said as she set the picture down. "I bet you can see this one though. This is my sister Lisa and Jack's wedding picture," she said, pointing to a large wall portrait. "This room used to be their room, you see, and when Jack moved to the garage apartment the picture stayed here. I think it was just too hard for him to look at after Lisa died."

"Your sister Lisa?" Raymie asked, confused.

"Yeah, my sister Lisa, the one who died."

Raymie moved close enough to peer at the large framed photograph. She could make out a much younger long-haired Jack in a white shirt open at the collar, with a dark vest and pants. Next to him stood a beautiful olive-skinned woman wearing a floor-length dress, a garland of flowers circling her dark hair. Despite the unconventional attire it was clearly a wedding picture, with the young couple holding hands and smiling happily into the camera. Raymie's forehead furrowed as she continued to look at the portrait. Then she said, "Oh. So, Jack is your brother-in-law?"

Marcie gave herself a playful slap on the forehead. "Jeez! That's right, he's my brother-in-law. I always forget to say the *in-law* part of it. He's been my brother for a long, long time, since he and Lisa got married when I was still in junior high. Then after I graduated high school, I came to live with them. I moved into the little apartment above the garage where Jack is now, but mostly I hung out in the house with Lisa and Jack and the boys." Marcie looked at the portrait. "We were one big happy family." She paused, frowning. "Well, mostly. It wasn't always perfect." Then she brightened up. "And we were a noisy bunch too, with two boys and our pets and everything. Everybody coming and going all the time and the boy's stuff piled all over the place. Not like now. Now it's pretty quiet."

"And now Jack stays in an apartment above the garage?"

"Uh huh. You see, after Lisa died Jack couldn't stand to be in their bedroom and so he was sleeping on the couch and I said, 'Why don't we trade?' And that's when I moved into their old bedroom in the house, this room right here, and Jack moved into the room above the garage." She looked around her. "It was quite a while ago that Lisa died but I don't remember how long. Jack could tell you, though." She shook her head sadly.

"He always knows exactly how long."

"I'm sorry," Raymie murmured.

"Yeah . . ." Marcie said, fiddling with a frilly pillow from her bed. "But we're getting over it." Then she looked at Raymie, the sadness in her voice now replaced with excitement. "Hey! I tell you what! Does Shainy like to play fetch? We have a big back yard. Want to take the dogs out there?"

"Sure! Let me check the time first, though." Raymie pressed a button on her watch and it gave her the time in an electronic voice. "I can stay another twenty minutes or so before I have to leave for my bus," she said, suddenly wishing she had not planned such a short visit.

"Don't worry about the bus. Me and Jack can give you a ride home."

"Thanks, Marcie, that's sweet of you, but I don't mind taking the bus. It keeps me independent."

"You're sure?"

"Absolutely."

The wind picked up just as Raymie was getting ready to leave, the summery late-September day turning quickly to chill autumn. Stifling a shiver, she felt the seep of sharp air through the cracks of the door where she stood with Marcie and the two dogs, calm now after their romp in the backyard. Raymie settled her coat resolutely over her shoulders and fastened the top button snug against her chin. "It's time to go, girl," she told Shainy, then looked up as she heard Jack enter the room.

He had neatened up a little, his shirt tails now tucked in, his hair less disheveled than earlier. "I was just going to make a snack for everybody," he told her, absently running a hand through his hair and mussing it again, making Raymie smile, "but it looks like you're getting ready to leave."

"Oh, thank you! That's so thoughtful of you, but I have to hurry to catch my bus," Raymie said, busying herself with Shainy's harness.

"We'd be happy to give you a ride."

Raymie hesitated, tempted.

"No, Jack," Marcie told him. "She doesn't want a ride. She wants to be independent."

"Oh. Well, it's nice to have met you," Jack said, a hint of reluctance in his voice as he added, "I'm sorry we didn't get to visit more."

His voice, Raymie noticed, was as smooth and resonant as the notes of a cello. She adjusted one of the harness straps in an attempt to hide the unexpected flush that warmed her face. "It was nice to have met you too," she murmured, not looking up from her task. Shep came to lean against her thigh, his tail wagging softly and Raymie gave him a little scratch behind an ear. He responded with a quick lick on her nose. She laughed, giddy, wiping the wet from his big tongue off her face. "Thank you, Marcie," she said, looking over at her. "And you too, Jack, for a lovely visit." She glanced at Jack, catching his eye, that brief contact enough to make her feel unreasonably happy.

Walking to her bus stop, Raymie felt loneliness, her some-time companion, catch up and walk beside her. Maybe it was the chill wind pulling at her coat and fluttering Shainy's ears, but she wanted to turn back, knock on Jack and Marcie's door and beg to be a part of what they were, to sit again at their kitchen table, enveloped in the warmth of their home.

10

AFTER RAYMIE LEFT, Marcie joined Jack in a snack of toast and peanut butter before heading to her room, Shep trailing behind her. Passing by the living room, Shep stopped to look at the front door. "Are you sad that our new friends are gone?" Marcie asked him. "Me too. Maybe they'll come back again another time." She hoped so; she had really wanted Jack to get to know her new friend. After all, Raymie was a real find. She was so little and pretty and light on her feet, kind of like Tinkerbell minus the wings.

Marcie opened her bedroom door. "Come on, let's watch the Dalmatian movie. You always like that one, don't you, big guy?"

Marcie picked up the remote on the side table next to her bed.

As she looked up her eyes focused on Jack and Lisa's wedding picture. They could get into some real fights sometimes, those two, but they sure did love each other.

Marcie tried not to think too much about what it was like after Lisa died, but talking to Raymie about it brought up the old memories. After Lisa's death the preparations for her Celebration of Life kept them busy for the first week, but when that was past, she and Jack were left sitting with their grief. They spent time together watching TV, not eating much of anything but snack foods, neither bathing nor doing housework. When it got late Marcie would trudge up to her apartment where she would crawl into her unmade bed. Jack slept on the couch in the living room, watching TV until he couldn't stay awake any more.

After a few days, Marcie got up one morning and heard the neighbor kids laughing on their way to school and a chipmunk scolding from a nearby tree, and she knew that it was going to be okay.

But Jack seemed to be going further and further into a slump. He was like a zombie roaming around the house. Marcie watched him as he stared at the TV set, glad that he would be going back to work soon.

On the evening of the day he was supposed to have returned to work, Marcie came over to the house to ask Jack how his day had been. She found him lying on the couch in a wrinkled t-shirt and sweatpants, a half-empty jar of peanut butter lying on the floor next to the couch with a spoon sticking out of it.

"How was your first day back to work, Jack?"

"Oh Marcie," he said. "I guess I didn't go." Jack sat up and put his head in his hands. He was unshaven and smelled like he hadn't had a bath in days. He got up, barefoot, and walked to the bathroom. When he came back out he lay back down on the couch, his knees folded to give Marcie room to sit on the other side.

Marcie didn't sit down. "So, are you going to go tomorrow?"

"I don't know," he muttered. "Maybe."

The next morning Marcie marched over to the house. She stood in front of the couch and told him, "Jack, it's time to get up."

Jack rolled away from her and pulled the blanket more

firmly over his shoulder.

She pulled at his arm, which he jerked away from her grip, so Marcie leaned close to his ear and yelled, "Get up, Jack!"

Jack rolled to a sitting position. "Shit, Marcie."

"Shit nothing. You have to go to work. Go get a shower. You're stinky."

Jack stumbled into the bathroom and Marcie heard the shower running as she made coffee and poured him a bowl of cereal.

Jack came to the table, his hair dripping wet. "You're gonna have to drive me to work this morning. I missed my bus dinking around with the likes of you," Marcie told him.

"Sorry, Marcie," Jack mumbled as he took a sip of the coffee that she'd set before him. And made a face. "This is awful! You never could make a decent cup of coffee."

"You make it then," Marcie told him.

Jack got up to make coffee, and as he watched it drip, decided to fry a couple of eggs. He got out the frying pan. "Do you want a couple eggs, Marcie?"

"You bet," she said. "Over medium."

As Jack turned to start the eggs Marcie blew out a sigh of relief.

After that Jack started to follow his old rhythm. He got up in the mornings and went to work, shopped for groceries and made meals, took out the trash and mowed the lawn. But he still seemed like kind of a zombie to Marcie, like he wasn't quite there. She tried different things to get him interested in life again: special treats, funny movies, but the best was the fluffy half-grown puppy one of her co-workers had to give up when she moved to a new apartment. "His name is Shep," she told the surprised Jack as she handed him the leash. "He needs you to take care of him."

Jack got better as time went on. He even was able to laugh again, but he still wasn't the same old Jack. Thinking about this, Marcie shook her head. She understood why Jack was sad about Lisa dying, they were all sad, but Jack took it really, really hard. It was almost as if there was something else that was part of the sadness, but she didn't know what. Maybe from something long ago, something he didn't want to talk about.

Shep gave her hand a nudge and she responded with a little scratch on his rump. "I don't know, Shep. I can't figure it out. Can you?" Shep stared at her, his tongue hanging out. Marcie laughed and pressed the remote. "No more thinking about sad stuff, boy. Let's watch our movie."

11
Seattle, Washington, 1959

Jack often thought of his early years in terms of before and after. He remembered the secure and simple days when he was small, sitting cross-legged in front of the TV with his brother Steven, watching Howdy Doody, while his mother, the ironing board set up in the living room to iron clothes as she watched, laughed along with her sons at something silly the puppet had done.

He remembered his father coming home, bringing the fresh wind of the outside world in with him while the light faded in the sky, smiling as he hugged and kissed their mother then turning his attention to Jack to ask about his day at school and scooping up four-year old Steven to give him a little tickle. Jack was in love with his life in a world that felt just right. It was like they were all, the four of them, singing together, the full sound of their voices blending to make the joyful song that was their family.

Then one of the voices started to fade. Jack knew it to be the most important voice of all: his mother. It was as if she was no longer singing the words and he turned to her only to see her moving quietly out of the room, humming the tune so that no one would take notice of her departure.

And then one day Jack came home from school and she wasn't there. His aunt Shirley was there instead, and when he asked where his mom was, she said that his mom was on a trip. "But she didn't tell us," Jack said over his brother's crying. He stood in the entryway, still in his coat, his lunch pail dangling from his fingers, not wanting to step forward into the empty house.

She was gone for about four months, Jack was later able to estimate. But to a six-year old it seemed forever. There was a hole inside of Jack that was there all the time, like an aching hunger. Nothing seemed to fill it, not the snacks that he ate or the soggy TV dinners his dad made or even the cookies that his grandma baked to make them feel better.

At school he couldn't look the other kids in the eye. He felt like he was the only one who didn't have a mom: he was so bad that his mother had left him. The only other child who didn't live with his mom was Eric. Eric lived with his grandma and anyone who was bold enough to ask was told that Eric's mom didn't live with him because she was sick. Was Jack's mom sick too? His whole body felt heavy and slow and his teacher kept having to make him pay attention. Jack continually found himself looking out the window of the classroom. He couldn't help it.

Their dad got quiet. The air that crept in with him when he came home from work felt heavy and stale. When they sat at the dinner table to eat, the presence of an empty chair was so painful that they began to eat in front of the TV instead.

Sometimes Jack heard the adults talking, snatches of conversation he wasn't meant to hear, like his dad on the phone talking to Jack's grandmother: "I know, Mom, but she wants to see them— Well, if you really think so . . . but what about the letters? She's not some kind of criminal or anything." Then his father sounded sad, resigned. "Okay, Mom, if that's what you think."

Nobody would talk to the boys about why their mother had left. Sometimes they'd blame each other saying, "If only you hadn't made her mad by spilling your milk," or "It's because you whined all the time," and they'd start pushing one another, and then later crying and holding each other in a sorrowful hug.

Then one time, Jack was in the kitchen while his aunt was visiting. She and his dad were sitting at the kitchen table drinking coffee. She said something like, "You have to pull out of it, Tom. There are more fish in the sea." His dad said, "You don't understand Shirley, she was the one, I don't want anyone else." Aunt Shirley said, "She was the one, Tom, but you have to let go now. She made her choice."

Jack, who had been quietly looking at the Sunday comics spread out on the kitchen floor, forgotten by the adults, spoke up. "Are you talking about my mom?" he asked. They both turned to look at him, their eyes narrowed in disapproval. Jack felt his stomach jump. He knew that he'd done something wrong, crossed some line.

After that he went back to acting like everything was fine, knowing that was what was expected of him. He lugged the unspoken words around with him like a burden he couldn't let go, making his steps slow and labored.

When the apple tree in their front yard had its first blooms Jack came home from school to find his mom there. She was standing in the living room with Jack's father and his aunt Shirley, Steven clinging to her leg and crying into the folds of her skirt, her hand gently cupping his head. When she saw Jack, she fell to one knee, moving Steven into the circle of her arms and then opening them to include Jack.

"Jack!" she cried. "Oh Jacky, I've missed you so much!"

He ran into her arms and she lay her head against his and he clung to her, all the tears he'd been holding for so long wetting her blouse as she kissed first him, then his brother, their two small bodies a jumble of damp heat in her arms. Somewhere above them his aunt was saying, "Don't you think that's a bit much, Marion, after all you've put these two boys through?" And his dad's voice saying, "Leave it be, Shirley she's home now, that's all that's important." Then Aunt Shirley said, "I'm getting my coat." Nobody said anything for a minute, then Jack heard his dad say, "Thanks again for all your help, Shirley."

Jack heard the front door close forcefully behind her and they were alone together, a family once more.

In the days that followed their mom was quieter than Jack remembered her, sweet and loving and apologetic. "I'm so sorry I put you kids through that," she said sadly. "You know I love you so much." She brushed the bangs out of Jack's eyes, promising that it would be better, while Jack's brother clung to her dress, sucking his thumb even though he was way too old to do that.

As they settled in together again Jack watched his parents and noticed that they were cautious with one another, their smiles for each other tenuous and small, and he knew that things weren't the same between them. Something fresh and essential was gone, and it would never be there again.

It took a while for their lives to get back to normal, but for Jack there was never again a sense of complete security. A stutter had developed in Jack's perception of his family, a hesitation where once there had been a flow. He'd tell himself, "Everything is fine" but then another voice would creep in, a voice of worry.

He watched his mother carefully, willing her to stay steady, to sing all the words of the family song clearly, her voice full and strong. It wasn't until a couple of years had passed that Jack was able to let it fall away, to drop his vigilance to become a typical grade school child, with only a little apprehension remaining in his manner, the lingering wariness in his eyes only perceptible to those who had known the same kind of pain.

12

THE NEIGHBORHOOD where Jack lived for the first thirteen years of his life had once been farmland. Over time it had evolved into a suburban area, retaining pockets here and there of yellowed fields and crumbling outbuildings, eyesores to the adults, an invitation to play to children. Jack's house had a Seattle address, but the reality was that the city itself was a long way distant and didn't seem like a part of their lives, with the exception of the times when the family would go on day excursions to the large department stores there.

Most of the houses in the neighborhood had huge yards, and Jack and his brother Steven's yard was the biggest, graced with tall trees whose uppermost branches hovered over the rooftops. Ramshackle and comfortable, their house was the oldest on the block, built in the late 1800's and probably the house that went with the farm that once spanned the area. It was a shingled two story with a covered porch and high narrow windows, its run-down character making it a place where Jack and his brother could play uninhibited by the constant parental harping a more pristine home would require.

A favorite activity Jack shared with his two best friends Mike and Isaac was tree climbing. Pooling their resources, they built a treehouse together—a tree platform to be exact, because it lacked both a roof and walls—between a pair of thick branches in the maple tree behind Jack's house.

During the warm months of summer Jack liked to go to the tree house and spend some quiet time reading, pausing occasionally to gaze past the leafy cover to the rooftops of the neighboring houses and the mountains beyond. The solitude he sought rarely lasted very long. His reading was interrupted more often than not by a request from one of the younger neighbor kids to make up a story.

"Hey Jack, do the pirate again!"

This request was from Jimmy, one of the younger kids who came to their house to play.

"Yeah, do the pirate!' another voice piped in. Jack looked down to see that Isaac's little brother Sam had made it partway up to the tree house. He'd just learned how to use the rope ladder last week and he was getting more confident.

Jack leaned against the trunk. "You mean Long John Silver or Captain Hook?"

"Long John Silver. We want to play Treasure Island!"

"Aw, you guys, we did that yesterday."

"So?" Jimmy said, waving around the thin branch he had just plucked from the tree, a perfect sword. "Let's play it again. It was fun! I want to be Jim again."

"Yeah, and I want to be . . ." Sam screwed up his face.

"You want to be the one I made up for you, Ezra Davies?" Jack suggested.

"Yeah, him! Tell us the story, Jack!"

Below, he heard the crack of a baseball bat. His brother and a couple of boys, more Jack's age than Steven's, were playing baseball on the makeshift diamond that they had set up in the backyard. Jack looked down as Steven was sliding into second base. It seemed kind of weird that Steven was playing with the older boys and Jack was stuck with the littler kids that were closer to Steven's age. But Steven was an ace baseball player, and Jack, well—everyone knew that Jack was no good at sports. He'd rather read and make up stories like he was going to do right now. Leaning forward to catch the attention of the two smaller boys he said, "Well, here's the story. Now you, Sam, you're a stowaway hiding in the cargo hold, okay?" Jack looked at Sam who was clinging fiercely to the tree. "Do you want me to help you up so you can be with me and Jimmy?" Sam nodded and Jack got down beside him and helped him reach his hand up to the next branch.

Jack looked at Jimmy. "And you, you're Jim Hawkins. You don't know that there's another boy on board until Long John Silver sends you down to check something in the hold."

As Jack unraveled the adventure he'd created using the setting of one of his favorite books the boys acted out their parts and Jack played the charming, mildly scary, conniving pirate. On other days he would do the same thing for kids his own age, responding to requests to create a verbal backdrop to their imaginary worlds, but he especially liked to play with his friends Mike and Isaac, who loved to read as much as Jack did. The three of them made up long complicated stories from their favorite books, competing for the most inventive plot twists.

Like most children during that era, Jack had many companions in his grade school years, brought together by their joy of discovering the world and their love of the outdoors, their own private domain, while fathers worked seemingly dull jobs and mothers sat inside with cups of coffee, absorbed by the myriad tasks of running a household and raising children.

Partly because of the size of the yard, partly because it was set in the middle of the block, and maybe because of his mom's peanut butter cookies, Jack's house was a favorite place for the neighbor children to convene. There was a pause, true, during their mother's absence and for a time after her return, as if the other mothers were afraid of their children being infected by the trouble that had come to Jack's family, but after a time the kids drifted back. Those early years held many moments of contentment, of unity. As young children they all played together like puppies, boys and girls a happy tumble, uncaring about nuances that would divide them later as they developed the habit of judgement and broke into groups that would exclude those considered different.

13

Jack, now thirteen, sat gazing out the window of his eighth-grade math class and hearing his own wistful thought: "Summer used to feel so much longer when I was a little kid." It was almost winter already, the world had gone still, the lumpy strip of grass between the school sidewalk and the street looking forlorn as Jack's eyes followed a car moving slowly down pavement grayed with rain. He sighed and turned his attention back to his math teacher, who was writing an equation on the blackboard.

Math was not Jack's best subject and he knew that he needed to pay attention. As he willed himself to concentrate on what the teacher was saying his hand absently traced the patterned surface of his desk where former students had gouged their initials. The school really should get some new desks, but nobody seemed to care about this old school anymore. It was an ugly place, all worn out in a way that made it gloomy and tired. He heard that they were going to tear it down and build a new school in a couple of years, but he would have moved on to high school by then.

The teacher was saying something about exponents, and Jack tried to remember what that was. He really did need to pay attention.

Eighth grade wasn't so bad, he thought, or maybe he had just gotten used to what it was like being in junior high school.

Last year, as a seventh grader and in the youngest group at school, Jack had hated being at the bottom of the pack, jostled by the more aggressive boys and ignored by the older girls who seemed sophisticated and aloof. It didn't help that he was skinny and small. "You're a late bloomer," his mother had said. "You get it from both sides of the family. Don't worry, you'll shoot up ahead of the other boys in no time." Yeah, and in the meantime, he was shorter than most of the girls. This year he was finally getting more mature, so it wasn't as bad as seventh grade when he always tried to be the last into the shower at gym class because he was embarrassed when he compared his body with those of the other boys his age. Thankfully the gym teacher didn't seem to mind. Maybe he'd been a late bloomer, too. Jack frowned. What a stupid phrase, late bloomer. Like he was some kind of flower, not a kid who was just pathetically immature.

He'd made a few new friends at this school, even had a girlfriend for a little while at the beginning of the school year, but Isaac and Mike were still his main and best friends, hanging out at each other's houses, playing card games and writing stories together, Jack making up plots, Mike creating funny scenes, and Isaac correcting their grammar. Jack smiled to himself. Isaac was such a dweeb, a really smart guy, his head always in the clouds. He made Jack and Mike look cool, which wasn't all that easy. Yesterday, Mike, crazy-man Mike, shaking his long hair that he wore all shaggy like the Rolling Stones, told Isaac, "You gotta lose that short hair, man, and nobody wears those shirts with button down collars anymore. Get a clue, Isaac." Leaning forward for emphasis, Mike added, "It's nineteen sixty-five, for crying out loud!" Isaac just pushed his glasses more firmly against his nose and said, "Okay."

That made Mike and Jack roll with laughter. He didn't know

why, it was just so funny. Isaac smiled at them indulgently, but then the next day came to school in a shirt that was actually pretty mod, with loose sleeves and a large spread collar like all the guys were wearing.

Remembering that, Jack chuckled softly, then realized he'd accidently drawn attention to himself.

"So, Jack. What did you get for an answer?" Jack looked up at his teacher hovering over him, then at the problem written on the blackboard. Oh crap. He really did need to pay attention.

When the last bell of the day had rung Jack joined Mike and Isaac in the hallway where lockers were being jerked open and banged shut as kids tossed in books and pulled out coats. As Mike was putting on his jacket, an older boy, a big stocky guy, bumped into his shoulder as he pushed past, not stopping to apologize. "Hey!" Mike said, his body stiffening with anger, fist balled, ready for a fight.

"Just let it go," Jack told him. "Remember next year we'll be the top dogs."

Mike blew out a breath, "Yeah, ninth graders at last."

"And I'll be able to take Chemistry!" Isaac told them.

Mike and Jack turned to look at Isaac. You had to love the guy, he really didn't have a clue.

"Right," Mike said, and he and Jack broke into laughter. Isaac joined them, catching on to the joke, and the three boys turned to begin their walk home in easy companionship.

When Jack got to his house the kitchen was warm from newly baked cookies. He had hung up his coat and had accepted the still warm cookies his mother had offered when his brother Steven, who now liked to be called Steve, burst through the door, cheeks red from the cold and maybe from tossing a ball back and forth with one of his buddies on the way home from school. The kid was all about sports—that's all he ever talked about.

"Steve," their mom said, "help yourself to a couple of cookies and come into the living room. I have something to talk to you boys about."

Jack's stomach dropped. He followed his mom into the living room. With the boys settled on the couch, their mother stood in front of them looking slightly nervous. "I have some exciting news, but there's going to be some changes for you boys, for all of us, actually," she said in a bright voice. "Your dad called me from work on his lunch break today. He got the new job he'd applied for!"

"Alright Dad!" Steve crowed.

Jack said, "Great!" But he remained apprehensive.

"It's at the new plant in Auburn, which is a long drive for your dad." His mom drew a breath. "So, this summer we'll move to a house that's closer to his work."

"Oh," Jack said, "but I kind of like this house." He could feel Steve, beside him on the couch, nodding his head in agreement.

"Oh, I know, boys, I like this house too, but we'll find a better one, a brand new one maybe, and it will feel like home in no time."

Something was just starting to dawn on Jack. "Will I have to go to a different school next year?"

"Well, yes Jack, but it's a nicer school than your junior high, and," she said, turning to Jack's brother, "your new school is really nice too, Steve. We've seen pictures of both schools and your dad and I are quite impressed.

Jack frowned. "But Mom, Steve will be in the seventh grade next year. Won't we be in the same school?"

His mom hesitated. "Actually, no, Jack—their high school

starts in the ninth grade. You'll be going to high school next year!"

"I'll be one of the younger kids again," Jack said, his voice flat. "Mom, I was really looking forward to being one of the older kids at my school. I was just talking about that with Mike and Isaac today." Jack stopped, further realization coming to him. Oh God. Mike and Isaac. What was he going to do without his two best friends?

His mom gave him a warning look. "You'll be fine, Jack. Your dad and I have already looked into it. These are both very good schools."

Steve, who had been quiet during this exchange only seemed to have one thing on his mind. He sat forward, asking eagerly, "What do you hear about the athletics department at my new school? I bet they have a good baseball team!"

Slumped in despair on his side of the couch, Jack groaned.

14

Jack looked at the typed slip of paper he was holding, then at the door in front of him. Room 102. The paper said his homeroom was in 202. That must be upstairs. He walked down the hall to a wide staircase, the steps worn by years of use. His mom had told him that this school was a lot better than his last, but Jack wasn't all that impressed. It was the same kind of brown two-story as his junior high, maybe a little less gloomy, but still not that much of an improvement. Maybe the teachers were better or something. Over his shoulder he heard someone say, "Hey Jack!" Turning, he saw that the guy wasn't greeting him. It must be a different Jack, he thought, as he heard another boy call out, "Hi Pete! How's it hangin' man?"

As Jack started up the stairs two girls were coming down on the opposite side, both wearing short dresses with puffy sleeves. One of them had piled on eye makeup, her blonde hair cut short like that model Twiggy. The girls glanced at him, curious, but neither said hi. In fact, no one at this school had said anything to him yet. Not a single person had said hi or asked him if he needed help, even though Jack was sure he looked lost. Everybody here seemed to know each other, and nobody appeared interested in knowing him. Sighing, he trudged up the stairs, dodging a group of boys coming toward him, talking and laughing, oblivious to the fact that they had crowded out Jack.

By the time he'd found his classroom the bell had already rung, which meant he had to walk in late, with the whole class staring at him. As he walked in the teacher looked at her attendance sheet and asked, "Jack Wallace?"

"Here," he said, feeling foolish. Were you supposed to say "here" in high school? Apparently that was the right thing because the teacher checked his name off on the attendance sheet and waved him to a seat near the back. Jack sat down, setting his notebook on the desktop, and began what would turn out to be a lonely first year at his new school.

P.E. class. You couldn't escape it. But finally, after weeks of humiliating himself in front of these kids he barely knew, fumbling footballs and serving volleyballs into the net, the teacher was holding a basketball when the class assembled on the gym floor.

Now here was something Jack could do. Well, not exactly catch the ball with any great success, but he could dribble, and for some inexplicable reason, he was good at shooting baskets.

The class tossed the ball from one to another, Jack missing his usual two out of three catches. Then they lined up to shoot baskets. Holding the ball, Jack crouched down, then sprang forward to hurl the ball toward the basket, where it made it through cleanly.

When it came to be Jack's turn again, he made another perfect basket. This time he heard one of the boys say, "Way to go, man," and he felt weeks of tension melt out of his body.

As Jack was tying his shoes, dressed and ready to go to his next class, his gym teacher approached him. "You surprised me today, Wallace." He said, "Who'd of thought a scrawny kid like you could shoot a basket like that?"

Jack shrugged, picked up his books.

"Have you thought of trying out?"

"Uh, no," Jack said, shifting the books in his hand.

"Well, you should."

Jack thought about trying out for the junior varsity team for several weeks, until basketball season was well past. His dad really wanted him to get involved in sports, always harping at him to join a team, but practice took so much time out of the day, time Jack would rather spend reading. But again, it might be a way to make friends, or at least to be around other kids. He wasn't a jock—the furthest thing from it, actually—and he didn't expect to have much in common with the other boys on the team.

In the time he'd been at this new school Jack had managed to strike up only one friendship—well, a friendship of sorts—with one of the guys in his social studies class. One day before class had started he overheard the guy, whose name turned out to be Joe, telling another student about the car that he was restoring. "Yeah," Joe was saying "it's a 1949 Chevy fastback. I figure I'll put in a V8 and paint it red."

"Hey," Jack said, the other guys turning to look his way, "that sounds pretty cool. My dad has an old 1938 Chevy coupe that he's going to let me have. I plan to start restoring it as soon as I get the money. Of course, there's no rush. I can't even get my learner's permit until next year."

"A '38?" Joe said. "Those are really cool, especially if you soup 'em up good. What you gonna do to it?"

"Oh, I was just thinking of restoring it to its original condition."

"No, man, you gotta soup it up. I've got some Polaroids in

my locker, shows what a buddy of mine did. Come find me at lunch and I'll show you."

At lunch Jack found Joe and his friends at the rear part of the cafeteria. "Sit down," Joe said, "I brought my pictures."

Jack sat down. After weeks of sitting alone at lunchtime or hanging out in the parking lot or the library to pass the time, Jack had someone to sit with. He feigned interest in the souped up hot rod that Joe was talking about and asked for his advice on the Chevy, even though he knew that he would never lower the chassis or paint flames on the side. After that he ate lunch with Joe and his friends every day, boning up on classic cars and car shows so that he would have something to talk with them about.

One afternoon the conversation turned to movies. Joe and his friend Pete had gone to see "Night of the Living Dead."

"Oh God, it was really gross," Pete was telling them. "It scared all the girls half to death, they were all screaming and stuff. There were these zombies walking around eating people, you know, blood smeared all over their faces." Reaching into his plate of leftover french fries, Pete smeared some ketchup around his mouth to demonstrate, curling his fingers into claws and pretending to chew on an arm.

"That's sick," one of the other guys said, laughing.

"It sounds a little bit like this story I'm writing," Jack said.

Several heads swiveled his direction. Jack realized that he'd probably made a mistake bringing it up, but thought, 'Oh well, why not?' and plunged ahead anyway. "It's about this plague that sweeps the earth and leaves everyone incapable of feeling emotion. That's really disastrous because moms ignore their babies, or even get rid of them if they cry too much, and people just let old folks who are like, senile, wander around in the streets, confused, until they die of exposure. Nobody feeds the poor or takes care of people who are sick." He paused, looking at the other kids' blank faces, knowing he was losing them. "Mankind is dying off because they don't care enough to do what they need to do to survive."

The other boys continued to stare at him. Jack felt the warmth of embarrassment start to creep up his neck. "But luckily, there are a few people who are immune to the disease and are still capable of feeling emotion. I haven't quite figured it out yet, but somehow they're going to save the day."

Joe looked at him suspiciously. "All that stuff about feelings makes it sound like some kinda girls' story."

Jack knew he'd made a mistake. This clearly wasn't the kind of story that Joe and his pals would appreciate. Reassessing his audience, he narrowed his eyes and leaned forward like he used to when he made up stories for the younger boys in his old neighborhood. "And all the guys get into these nasty fights, see, and just tear each other up, ripping off body parts and leaving the dead bodies in the street like garbage"—he thought fast—"and the bodies rot and stink like hell and there's this gross yellow puss just oozing out of their eyes."

"Cool," Joe said, drawing the word out, "and maybe the old people, they could be like zombies walking around all crazy."

"Yeah." Jack took a breath and leaned back in his seat in relief. He felt mildly disgusted with himself for changing the story but he was also disgusted with the other guys for being more interested in gore than ideas about human emotion.

Mike and Isaac would have loved the story exactly how he'd written it. It was an interesting idea, whether or not the human race could survive without having feelings. They wouldn't think it was dumb. God, how he missed those guys.

Jack had kept contact with Mike and Isaac through letters

and an occasional long-distance phone call, but it seemed like they were drifting apart. Mike told him that Isaac had met some new friends and he and Mike didn't hang out much anymore. Mike had a girlfriend now, and he spent a lot of his time with her instead.

Jack could tell that his friends were getting on with their lives, and that he was no longer part of them. After the first couple of months the frequency of the letters and phone calls dropped off. Since then the loneliness he'd felt had become a constant dull ache.

Feeling less comfortable with Joe and his crowd all the time, Jack noticed that his brother was making friends quickly. Steve had tried out for baseball and was going to practice several times a week, often stopping at the local Dairy Queen with his team afterward. Maybe this was what Jack should do: join a team. It couldn't be any worse than hanging out with Joe and his cronies, who, if he was to be honest with himself, really only tolerated his presence at their lunch table.

One night at dinner he thought to himself, 'Oh, what the hell,' and told his family, "I think I'm going to try out for basketball next year."

His mom looked at him in disbelief. His dad set down his fork. "That's the best idea you've had in a long time, son!"

The next year Jack tried out for the junior varsity team. He wasn't all that crazy about the game, but he liked the fact that his dad showed more interest in him and he liked to see his parents, whose relationship sometimes still felt tenuous, come together to watch the games, his mom clutching her purse to her, carefully navigating the bleachers to find a good spot to sit, his dad following behind her, talking excitedly, scanning the gym for a glimpse of their son.

The other guys on the team seemed to accept Jack, but they didn't feel like his crowd any more than Joe and his buddies did. Nobody did, really. He copied their jocular manner and went out with them for pizza or a burger after their games, even dated one of the guys' sisters for a while, but no close friendships emerged. Their easy camaraderie didn't dispel his loneliness and he considered himself a fake, someone playing a role. Jack figured that was just how it was. He didn't seem to fit in anywhere anymore, so he just had to pretend to be like the others. He supposed it was better than having no friends at all.

15

SLIDING INTO his desk in Mr. Okato's English class, Jack bumped his right knee against the underside of the desktop. "Ow!" he said under his breath as he rubbed the knee. Great. It would be a huge bruise later, just in time for basketball practice to start up again. As if he didn't already look dorky enough in his uniform, all knobby knees and big feet. He'd grown a lot during the summer, and even though he liked his new height, he was having a hard time managing his gangly limbs.

Shrugging it off, he opened the folder he'd set on the desk to find the handout Mr. Okato had given the class yesterday: "The Mechanics of Poetry." Over the past several weeks he had assigned them to read a mixed selection so they could experience a range of poetry styles. Jack's favorites were e. e. cummings and Dylan Thomas, each very different in the forms they chose to use, but similar in their ability to evoke clear, fresh imagery.

Mr. Okato had also taught them about stanzas, meter and rhyme and had even read them a poem he'd written himself.

Jack loved this class. Mr. Okato—or "Mr. O" as they called him—made English, already Jack's favorite subject, completely engrossing. Mr. O exuded energy; he was a vigorous, muscled, not-very-tall guy only a handful of years older than his students. The classroom rules were lax as long as they paid attention.

He allowed gum chewing, slouching and doodling during his lectures, and somehow he managed to make bored, restless teenagers into students who cared about classic literature and creative writing.

As the last of the arriving students settled into their desks, Mr. O got up from his chair and cleared his throat. The class slowly hushed, their eyes trained on their teacher.

"You've had a chance to read some poems and learn about structure. Now it's time to put that knowledge to use. I'm giving you the weekend to come up with a poem of your own," he said, scanning the upturned faces in the room, "so let's get creative!"

Jack noticed one of the girls, not very attractive but smart, that he had dubbed "the sketching girl" because she was always drawing things, nod with interest as she pushed aside her sketch to look attentively at Mr. Okato, and he heard a guy in the next row back murmur, "Far out man!"

There were also groans from some of the boys in the back row, one of them a guy who was on his basketball team.

Jack held in his excitement. He had been writing poetry ever since he was introduced to the form as a small boy listening to his grandmother read from a book of children's poetry. The only people he'd ever shown his writing to, besides his mom, who was his best advocate and a gentle critic, were Mike and Isaac. Now that they had faded from his life Jack had no one other than his mother to share his poems with. He had taken to hiding them away in his room for fear of being misunderstood or teased.

Later that day at home in his bedroom, Jack agonized over the assignment. Should he write something pretty lame just like most of the other guys would? He looked through the sheaf of handwritten poems that he had scribbled on various sheets of paper at different times over the past several years, then stashed away in a folder on the top shelf of his closet. No, he didn't want to write something lame; he wanted other people to hear his poems.

Here was a favorite that described how he felt when he was hanging out with the other guys on the team. He pulled it out of the pile and read it silently to himself:

> I guffaw, I bray, I mimic faithfully
> In sacrifice of self, a coarse camaraderie.
>
> A slap on the back, a punch on the arm
> The shallow rites to prove I belong.
>
> I bend, I pose, I play the part,
> Within this role hides my heart.
>
> And still I'm all alone.

Jack considered the poem. He liked it, but felt like it revealed too much about himself.

What if he changed the "I" to a "he?" He got out the dog-eared thesaurus he had found at a second hand store and spent the next several hours revising the poem, trying this word and that to find the best fit.

The next day he picked up the new, much-revised version off his desk and read it over.

The Actor

A guffaw, a bray, he mimics faithfully
In sacrifice of self, a coarse camaraderie.

A slap on the back, a punch on the arm,
Shallow rites he performs to belong.

He bends, he poses, he plays the part
Sensitivity censored, he hides his heart.

And still he stands alone.

Yes, that was better. Jack read the poem over a couple more times, and was satisfied with the changes. He was even kind of proud of it and he had a feeling that Mr. O might be impressed.

He went to find his mother and asked if he could use her typewriter.

On Thursday of the next week, Mr. Okato stood in front of the class with their assigned poems in his hand. He held them up, saying, "Several of these are pretty good. You'll see that most of my corrections are for grammar and mistakes in format. I've also given you suggestions for improvement where needed." He looked down at the pile of papers. "I'm going to read you a couple of these that show real promise. This first one is especially good."

And then he read Jack's poem aloud to the class.

Jack felt stunned, barely able to hide the tremor that went through his body as he heard his work read. It seemed like his vision had been funneled to only include Mr. Okato standing there with the paper in his hand.

When he was finished Mr. Okato was silent a moment, just as he was after he read the poetry of the great poets that they'd learned about in class. Then he said, "Good job, Jack, nice use of alliteration. Keep it up. You have talent."

Mr. O. handed the poem to Jack. As Jack reached out to take it, he saw that most of the class had turned to look at him. The guy from his team looked puzzled, or maybe disgusted, he wasn't sure. A couple of the girls smiled at him, among them the sketching girl, who turned out to be the person whose poem Mr. Okato would read next. One guy, a new guy, named Adam or Andrew or something like that, nodded his approval, giving him a thumbs up.

The class broke for lunch. Jack picked up his books, mentally practicing what he would say to the guys that he always ate lunch with, who were mostly jocks from his basketball team and included Tom, the guy who looked at him with that weird expression after his poem was read. Jack was thinking that if anyone asked, he would pretend that the poem was something a cousin of his had written and had let Jack use. The poem was just too close to how he felt about those guys to admit the truth. Jack shrugged to himself. It really was a shame that he felt the way he did about his teammates. They weren't bad people, he liked them in a general way, but they were a poor substitute for the kind of friendships he once had with Mike and Isaac.

The new student, the one who had given him the thumbs up, was waiting for him outside the classroom.

"I liked your poem, man," he said, falling into step with Jack. "I know exactly what you're getting at there."

Jack regarded him with interest. The guy continued. "I feel

that way a lot myself. All those rules about what it means to be a man. There is this real pressure to suck it in, adhere to the standard." He shook his head of long dark hair. "It's suffocating."

"Oh. Actually, that poem really wasn't about me."

The guy rubbed his chin, looking sideways at Jack. "Yeah. Right."

Jack glanced at the other boy, whose shaggy hair exceeded the dress-code length, a stray wavy strand falling forward to partially shield one lens of his John Lennon-style glasses. His appearance reminded Jack of the hippies that he'd read about in the paper. The Woodstock rock festival had made international news just a few months before and he remembered seeing the people that had come to this rock and roll mecca on the evening news, standing in the pouring rain together, swaying to the mesmerizing music being played on the glowing altar of the stage before them.

He saw some hippies in Seattle the last time he was there with his family. They looked relaxed and happy in their colorful clothes and long hair, lounging about in the park while Jack and his family sat stiffly at their picnic table. Some of them were playing music, others dancing in abandon, alone or together in a creative free-form style.

From what he'd heard, they were opposed to war and believed that every person had value. Jack had liked those ideas, wanted to know more.

The other student stopped and turned to Jack. "My name's Arjun." Seeing Jack's look of curiosity, he shrugged. "I know, unusual name, right? I'm named after an uncle who lives in Calcutta. My mom's from India. My dad met her when he was teaching over there.

"Do you like to read, Jack?"

Jack felt a smile pulling at his lips, "Do I like to read?" He said, pretending to mull it over. "Let's see . . . Is the pope Catholic?"

"Far out, man," Arjun said, flipping the hair off his face with a shake of his head. "I really like to read too. What are you reading right now?"

"I've been reading this book called 'One Flew Over the Cuckoo's Nest,'" Jack told him. "It's an amazing story. Really well-written. The author is Ken Kesey—have you heard of him?"

"Ken Kesey? Sure, he's really trippy. Have you read 'The Electric Kool-Aid Acid Test?'" Arjun looked at Jack, who shook his head.

"It's written by Tom Wolfe, this really *insane* cultural satirist. It's about Kesey and these guys who travel around with him all over the country in a tripped-out bus blowing people's minds with all kinds of crazy antics. Very iconoclastic." Arj pulled a book out of his book bag. The title was "Cat's Cradle." "I've been reading this guy named Kurt Vonnegut. Have you read any of his stuff?"

Jack frowned. "The name sounds familiar."

"My favorite is the one written back in 1952 called 'Player Piano.' I'll lend you a copy if you want. You can borrow this one too when I'm done with it if you're interested."

Jack felt a growing excitement. It had been a long time since he'd had a conversation like this. "I'm definitely interested. Maybe I have some you'd like to borrow."

Arjun cocked his head, looking at Jack speculatively. "I'm going to the vacant lot to smoke a J. Want to come with me?"

Jack's coach strictly forbade the use of drugs or alcohol, but Jack had tried marijuana once at a party and enjoyed the mellow high he got from it. He hesitated. "I guess so, but I can't get too wrecked. I have a biology test fifth period."

"No worries man, this is just leaf."

Not really understanding what Arjun was referring to. Jack followed him to the wooded vacant lot adjacent to the school. They joined several other students huddled over cigarettes and small wooden pipes. Bob, who played center, was just stubbing out a cigarette. Before leaving he put a finger to his lips to caution Jack against telling their coach.

Arjun produced a joint from his shirt pocket, lit it and inhaled deeply. "How long have you been writing poetry?" he asked as he passed it to Jack.

"Since I was a little kid." Eyeing the lumpy yellow-tinged object in Arjun's hand Jack tried to remember how to smoke it. He took it from Arj and held it carefully between his thumb and forefinger as he'd seen the other boy do.

"Just take a long hit," Arj said casually, "and hold it as long as you can."

Jack drew in the smoke, held it in his lungs for as long as he could stand it, then exhaled, coughing and laughing at the same time.

Arjun's laugh joined his, the joyful sound of one bouncing off the other until it felt to Jack that the laughter was taking on a life of its own. His thoughts drifted off as he stood gazing up at the trees, lost in their leafy glory. "Wow," he said, catching his breath. "I feel really good right now."

"Right on, man," Arjun said, taking another toke. "Yeah, it's pretty good pot."

"Oh, well, yeah, it does seem pretty good. But I don't really think it's the pot. It's . . . I mean, I feel . . ." Jack closed his eyes looking for a way to explain. "I feel like myself," he said, nodding. He started to get teary, waved away the offer of another toke. "I feel like myself," he repeated, full of wonder, and—what was this? Joy?

"Not The Actor anymore, huh?"

"No." Jack took a deep breath. "I'm sick of The Actor." He smiled. "Oh. And I actually did write that poem about myself."

Arjun gave Jack a wry grin. "I know."

Jack laughed, and felt every muscle in his body loosen with the comfort of finding home within himself once again.

Before they parted ways to go to their classes, Arjun told Jack about Stuart, a friend he'd met over the summer when Arjun's family moved next door to his. The boys got to talking and found out that they both played guitar and so they started jamming together with a third guy who played keyboard. After school started up again, Stuart, who was an honors student and had the favor of his teachers, was able to finagle the use of the music room for band practice twice a week after school.

"We're actually not playing that much," Arjun told Jack. "We're mostly hanging out. Other kids drift in and we all just talk about books, read the stuff we've written, maybe play a few guitar riffs to sing along with, that kind of thing. Drop by if you want to."

A couple of days later Jack was poking around the hallway, looking for the music room when he heard Arjun call out, "Jack! Hey man, come join us!" Arj poked his head out of a door and Jack walked over.

As he entered the room, Arjun was telling the others, "This is Jack, the guy I was telling you about, who wrote that poem."

"Cool," one of guys said, and walked over to shake Jack's hand. "I'm Stuart," he said, "and this is our gang of merry pranksters." Stuart waved an arm toward the rest of the kids assembled there. Besides Arjun and Stuart, there were two other boys and a couple of girls. One of the girls was sitting on top of the baby grand with her legs dangling off the side, a pad of paper in her lap. The sketching girl from Mr. O's class. Of course. She nodded at him in recognition. "I'm Sam, or, Samantha," she said, giving a little shrug. "And this is Cheryl." She tipped her head to indicate the pretty dark-haired girl in a short skirt and fringed jacket standing next to a guy with red hair wearing a paisley shirt. "I'm Nick," the red-haired boy said, putting a possessive arm around Sheryl.

Jack turned to the remaining boy, who was sitting on the teacher's desk, long hair tied back into a messy ponytail. "Phil," he said, "Good to meetcha, Jack. Welcome to our motley crew."

16

GROUPED ON THE scratchy brown sectional sofa in their living room, Jack and his parents were watching the evening news. The news anchor told of the latest protest march as the camera panned the surge of people moving down the streets of Seattle, men and women, most of them young, some of the guys in military jackets and faded jeans, headbands around their long hair, fists raised, shouting, "Hell no, we won't go!"

Jack's dad got up and switched the channel, his movements sharp with distaste.

"Tom," Jack's mom said, leaning forward as if to switch the news back on. "We were watching that."

"I'm sorry, Marion, but I just can't stomach it. My sister's boy Rob is happy to serve," he told her. "He's proud to wear the uniform of the United States Marine Corps, not like these young ... *rebels* who are protesting the war. Did you know that in some places they're spitting on returning soldiers?"

"Well, that's just wrong, and we both know that," Jack's mom said. "But look, Tom, have you talked to your sister lately? The last time I talked to Joyce she told me Rob is not doing very well. He had to take medical leave for battle fatigue. You know, shell shock? Whatever you call it, he's pretty badly shaken up. She says he just wanders around the house, nervous and confused."

"Rob's tough—he'll get over it."

"Joyce says he's having nightmares. He told her that it wasn't what he expected. He doesn't want to go back."

"Well, I can't believe that."

Jack's mom nodded. "I was surprised to hear it too. This isn't like Rob, he's always been such a solid kid, nothing ever seemed to faze him. And, you know, the fact that if even a boy like Rob was affected so badly, well, that tells me that there might actually be something to what these young people are saying about this war." She ran her hand through her dark hair, looking thoughtful. "I've been thinking a lot about this, and what I've come to realize, is that this isn't like the second world war. We had a good reason to fight that one, and everyone was happy to do their part. Young men rushed to enlist back then, but it's not like that now." She paused to gather her thoughts, and Jack, sitting next to her on the sofa looked at his mother in surprised admiration. He rarely saw her so fired up. "At the very least," she continued, "they should abolish the draft for this war. These boys shouldn't be *forced* to go."

"Steve wants to go," their dad said, referring to Jack's younger brother. "He talks about it all the time."

"Steve's young yet. It's Jack who might have to go. He'll have to sign up for the draft in less than a year."

"Best thing for him. It'll make him into a man."

"That's right, Tom, a *dead* man. Is that what you want?"

"Oh, for crying out loud, Marion. You always exaggerate things."

The remnants of their school lunches set aside, Jack and his friends Stuart and Arjun huddled at their table to talk about Vietnam, their heads bent together to form a circle of shared concern.

"My neighbor Eric got his draft card," Stuart was telling them. He says he's real freaked out because his sister went to 'Nam as a nurse and she said that it was like living in hell. She told Eric he should refuse to go."

"She's got a point there," Arjun said. "None of the guys I know want to fight this war. I've been hearing that some of them are going to Canada, like this friend of my brother's. He went there when his draft notice came through and he's living in the woods somewhere, hiding out."

"Well, I don't know, you guys," Jack said cautiously. "Not that I'd consider it, but my dad keeps telling me I should enlist after I graduate. He says it's a lot better than being drafted, and the army would give me a really good deal, letting me pick my own job, and then paying for my college when I get out."

The normally unflappable Stuart turned on him. "Come on Jack! Haven't you been paying attention? Don't you remember what happened to Samantha's brother?"

"Samantha?" Jack said, surprised by Stuart's anger. "Our friend Samantha? I didn't even know she had a brother."

"Lay off, Stuart," Arjun said. "Of course Jack doesn't know about Samantha's brother. That was a couple of years ago, before Jack even knew all of us. After what happened, she just stopped talking about him." Arjun turned to Jack. "You see, man, Samantha's brother enlisted, just like what your old man is talking about. He thought he would get a good deal, but they just sent him right into the middle of the fighting."

Stuart picked up the story. "Her brother sent letters home to their folks saying everything was fine, but the letters he sent Samantha were different. She used to read them to us. He was going through hell. Horrible things were happening and nobody seemed able to stop it. All around him he saw people losing faith in the war and in our government. A lot of the guys in his platoon were taking drugs, shooting up heroin and whatever else they could get their hands on, just so they could stop thinking about it for a while."

"Was her brother killed there or something?"

"You got it," Arjun told him. "The poor sucker came home in a box."

"Oh God," Jack breathed, "I didn't know. That's really sad."

Stuart looked at his two friends. "Listen, we're all planning to go to college, right? It's a simple thing to take a college deferment. We won't even have to think about the draft for four whole years, and by then, the war might be over."

17

WHEN BASKETBALL SEASON rolled around again Jack surprised himself by joining the team for a second year. He hadn't planned to; now that he had his new group of friends he didn't need it to assuage his loneliness, but there was something about the slap of tennis shoes on the gym floor and the easy comradery of his teammates that pulled Jack away from the nagging worries about the war and kept him in the concrete world. His schoolwork, his part time job at the local grocery and basketball all helped him to sink into the illusion of a world that was normal and secure, a Norman Rockwell version of a boy's adolescence, marked by confidence and industry, devoid of the uncertainty that lurked just below the surface.

Then, after the drenching rains of spring, the school year ended and summer came on clear and hot. Jack felt a loosening of the anxiety that seemed to always be right at his elbow, to remember that he was young and that this was the last summer of his youth, a time to be free and joyful.

Seattle's Seward Park sponsored rock music at the amphitheater every Saturday that summer. Jack and several of his friends all squeezed into Cheryl's mother's gargantuan station wagon, as many as eight or nine at a time, the cramped quarters buffered by the homemade blackberry wine she had pilfered from her grandfather's musty basement, easy going down with a distinctive acidic burn coming back up.

Cheryl was at the wheel when she left home with a reasonable cargo of five or six kids. Unknown to her mother, she would pick up a few more later, handing over the wheel to any of them willing to stay reasonably sober for the long trip to the city.

At the end of the drive, they emerged from the car wrinkled and sweaty but eager to follow the heart thrum of the music that they could hear as they trudged up the path to the amphitheater. The path opened to the scene before them, the pounding music, the twirling bodies, people lounging everywhere on blankets or in the sweet-smelling grass, joints passed randomly from hand to hand. It was a free-for-all carnival where each person in attendance was both audience and performer.

Jack and his friends invariably chose to join the swaying bodies closest to the stage. Everyone was moving, some dancing with large wild movements, others linking arms to whirl in a circle. It was all abandon, all freedom, all joy, marred only by the people on bad trips who wandered among them, the skinny runaways looking for spare change, the lecherous older guys who grabbed young girls in a lurching sexual hold, and the occasional puke over a log as the blackberry wine, augmented by greasy vendor food, made its way to the surface.

Late in July, Jack found himself next to a barefoot girl dressed in a patterned skirt with only a knotted scarf covering her small breasts. Her dance was elaborate and alluring, the sexuality in her swaying hips in frank display.

"I'm Camilla," she told Jack in a dry, whispery voice when there was a break in the music. She spread her arms wide above her head to encompass everything around her. "Don't you just love this?"

"This is amazing," Jack agreed.

"Dance with me," she commanded as the music started again, and Jack moved his feet self-consciously, grateful that she had abandoned herself to the music and his half of the dance didn't really matter.

When the music slowed to a ballad, she said to him, "Do you want to take a walk with me?"

Jack looked around for his friends so that he could tell them where he was going.

"Don't worry about them," she said, taking his face to turn it toward her. "They are free spirits, as we all are. Let them be."

Glancing behind him, Jack followed Camilla out of the crowd, her barefoot steps light on the path into the woods. The clearing she brought him to was fragrant with smooth, soft cedar needles.

"This is a good spot," she said. "Do you like this spot?"

Something was happening and he felt his body respond, alert and urgent.

She took off her skirt and spread it over the needles, then lay down on her side. He got down beside her, not quite sure what to do. She laughed softly, a series of three high tinkling notes. "Let me help you. Have you done this before?"

He shook his head and she said, "Ooh! How sweet!" before she pulled him on top of her, reaching confidently for the zipper of his jeans.

When Jack returned to the amphitheater, his friends were frantic. "Where did you go, man?" Arjun asked. "We were looking all over for you. It's time to head back. Cheryl's mom needs the car to take her little sister to cheerleader practice or something." Jack looked around for Camilla, who had disappeared into the crowd after promising to catch up with him the next weekend.

He followed his friends to the car, dazed, telling himself that what had just happened couldn't possibly have been real. Crammed into the back seat, his friends around him singing along with Janis Joplin on the radio, he looked out the window in amazement, replaying the memory. It had been different from what he'd expected, but absolutely... He couldn't find the right words. He watched as they passed by the blur of houses and trees, poised for the next experience the world would show him, his mind suffused with wonder.

He saw Camilla again two weeks later. She was wearing the same wide skirt, this time with a peasant blouse tucked in at her tiny waist, the scarf now tied around her head. He had told Arjun and Stuart about her, telling them not to worry if he left the group for a while.

"Hey, you!" she said, and Jack realized that she'd never asked his name. She began dancing, swaying her hips close enough for him to reach out and put a hand on her hip. She twirled away, seemingly unwilling to be captured, then beckoned for him to follow.

This time the clearing was occupied by a couple with similar ideas. She led him deeper into the woods where they found a less satisfactory spot close to a hiking trail. As she lay her skirt on the ground Jack had the fleeting thought that they might get in trouble. He wasn't sure that having sex in a park was legal, even though there seemed to be a number of people who were doing it.

Later, lying with her on her wide skirt he touched the dampness on her thigh, wondering if they shouldn't be holding hands or something. He was just about to reach for her hand when she sat up and stretched. "My friends and I belong to a commune in the Freemont district," she said in her odd whispery voice. "We run a bakery that sells natural, healthy food. Everything good for your body and soul! My friend Mark has a card with the information about the commune on it. You can come visit me there."

Camilla found her friend among the dancers. He fished a creased business card out of his back pocket and handed it to Jack. Before she walked off with a girlfriend who had asked Camilla to go with her to the restroom, Jack told her, "My name is Jack."

Camilla emitted her high tinkling laugh. "Good to know you, Jack. Come visit us anytime."

18

JACK WASN'T SURE why he had decided to come see the commune. He supposed it was curiosity more than anything else, and who knows? A lot of people were talking about communes, how wonderful they were. Maybe it would be something he should check out for himself. Maybe it would be better just to experience life for a while, live in a commune and spend his time writing poetry instead of starting college right away.

The bus ride to Seattle was long and sticky, and he wished his car didn't need new brakes before he could drive it again. He transferred from downtown to the Freemont district, getting off at the main business area. He asked around for the bakery and a man who wore his head in long twisted strands pointed Jack toward a brightly painted storefront on the main road.

The rich smell of yeast was intoxicating. There was a man in an untended beard behind the counter, his sleeves rolled to his elbows, showing sinewy arms, his hands dusted with powdery flour.

"Welcome!" the man said. "What can I do for you?"

"I'm looking for Camilla," Jack said. "A guy named Mark gave me a card?"

"I think Camilla's upstairs," the man behind the counter said. "Follow me."

Jack followed him up some narrow, steep stairs to the rooms on top of the building. There was a carpeted hallway with several doors opened to reveal cluttered rooms with mattresses and bedding spread on the floor, several to a room, the windows covered by brightly patterned cloth. Camilla was in one of the rooms, sitting cross legged, trimming the ends of the long hair of a girl sitting in front of her.

"Hi Jack!" she said, setting down the scissors and patting the other girl's shoulder to signal that they were done. She got lightly to her feet. "Welcome! Let me show you around."

She showed him the rest of the upstairs rooms. The largest one, the one in the front of the building that overlooked the street, had been devoted to a communal kitchen and dining area with a long rough table flanked by mismatched chairs. Several large overstuffed couches in varying stages of decline lined the walls on the other end of the room accompanied by coffee tables that overflowed with books, record jackets and soiled dishes.

"Everything here is shared," she told him. "We've freed ourselves from the burden of ownership. Isn't it beautiful?"

Jack made sounds of agreement although he was a little disappointed. The word *commune* evoked for him someplace closer to nature, surrounded by grass and trees, maybe a stream to wade in. These rooms were too warm, the close air mixed with the smell of something spicy and strange cooking on the stove, the yeasty smell of bread, with an undercurrent of pot and stale sweat.

"Lunch is nearly ready," someone announced. Jack recognized Mark, the guy who had given him the business card at the park. "Tear off a piece of bread. There's butter and jam, and the bowls for the stew are right over here."

Several other people filed in, reaching for bowls and standing in a loose line to dip some stew out of the large pot on the stove. Jack found a chair among them and Camilla sat next to him. "What do you think, Jack?" she said, her whispery voice close to his ear. "I talked to Mark, and there's a spare bed where Sonja was sleeping. She left to go back to her family on the east coast yesterday. It's yours if you want it."

Jack looked at her in surprise. "Oh. Thanks, but, I mean, I'm only seventeen."

The tinkling laugh again. "Sonja was only fifteen. Everyone is welcome, there's no age limit. We even had a woman here in her sixties for a while who was studying plant medicine."

Jack stabbed at an unfamiliar vegetable. He loved the crusty whole grain bread these people made, but the stew was strange, no meat, unusual spices and a mix of grains that he had no name for.

They got up to wash their dishes in the large double sink. A guy that Jack had noticed at the table came up and said something softly to Camilla. "I'll be back in a while," she said, putting the damp dishcloth on top of the pile of clean dishes.

Jack finished washing his bowl before going to the open window, where a street band was set up on the corner singing the war protest song that was so popular that year. The lyrics were filled with a loony sarcasm that carried an edge of hysteria, speaking to the sense of futility felt by those who would be forced to fight. A small crowd had gathered, clapping their hands and singing along. At the edge of the crowd was an older man in a uniform who was frowning. Clearly upset, he turned to the woman standing beside him and took her arm as they walked away.

Watching, Jack thought about his cousin Rob, who had been

so proud to serve. Rob had been treated for battle fatigue and sent back to the front. Jack hoped he was doing okay. God, this whole thing was just so messed up.

As he heard the last strains of the song, Jack saw a lone leaf drift off one of the young trees that lined the street, yellow with the promise of fall, and realized that school would be starting again in a few weeks. He needed to get back to the college applications sitting on his desk at home, and then there was the entrance exam coming up soon.

Mark, who was standing next to him, said, "Get your draft card yet, kid?"

"No, not yet, but I'm going for a college deferment."

"Smart idea," Mark said. "Some of the guys here are hiding out. If they're caught it's time in the slammer."

Jack turned to look around the room. "I have to get going soon. I probably should say goodbye to Camilla."

"Sorry man, she's off with David right now. She'll be back in a while, though. If you want to hang around, you're welcome to crash here tonight."

Jack wondered if he should be jealous, and then realized he didn't really care. "No, that's okay," he said, turning back to the window. "Thanks anyway, but I gotta get back." He took a deep breath, pushed it out. "There's a lot of stuff I need to take care of at home."

19

Poulsbo, Washington, October 2013

SOMETHING ABOUT the visit with Marcie and Jack stayed with Raymie. Her mind kept turning back to the memory of her short time there, brushing the images with a warm light, a glow of sorts. Nothing special stood out, really; it had been a typical mood-swing autumn day, from sun to wind and rain and back to sun again, but the cozy welcome she found sitting in their kitchen buoyed her up in the days that followed. Marcie and Jack and their shaggy, slightly smelly dog took on the form of a fairy-tale memory, a little too sweet perhaps, but appealing. This unlikely pair of people seemed to have forged such a satisfying life together, continuing a story line that managed to survive beyond the loss of its central character: Marcie's sister, Jack's wife.

On a morning not long after her visit with Marcie, Raymie was on her usual bus trip to her daughter's house in Seattle to stay with her grandson Aaron for the day while her daughter Allison ran errands. A few months shy of his fourth birthday, Aaron was such a delight, still in love with the world and the creatures in it, fascinated by the smallest things, and given to exclamations of joy over anything that pleased him, be it a sticky slug or the bright color of a dandelion.

Raymie's son-in-law, however, Aaron's dad Kyle, was a

disappointment. So charming at first, he turned out to be a selfish, critical man, very much like Allison's stepfather, Raymie's deceased husband Bill. Raymie saw with resentment how dismissive Kyle was of her wonderful daughter's accomplishments, focusing instead on her faults, and magnifying every small mistake. Allison didn't want to talk about it, forcing Raymie into the position of having to pretend everything was fine with Allison's marriage. She hated having to participate in that: it reminded her too much of her life with Bill, the way she always had to try to stay cheerful, to rise above his gloom, while constantly walking on eggshells, afraid of drawing his derision. Seeing Allison with a man like Kyle brought up such feelings of guilt. Did I do that? Raymie asked herself. Did I teach my daughter that my relationship with Bill was how a marriage should be? She sighed, turning her head to look out the window. She didn't want to think about it anymore.

Shainy, lying beside Raymie's seat on the swaying floor of the bus, gave a little groan, her head down between her front paws as if to echo Raymie's mood. Raymie leaned forward to scratch the back of Shainy's neck and she moved her head a little to help Raymie find the best spot, then abruptly lifted it as the bus slowed to a stop. She stood up and leaned against Raymie's leg, panting softly.

Marcie stepped up into the bus. "Hi Bob!" I heard her say to the driver. "How are you today?"

"Doing good, Marcie, doing good. And you?"

"Doing great!" she said, "and I see that my friends are here." She looked in Raymie's direction. "Hi Rainy! Hi Shainy!"

The bus started to move again as she plopped sideways into the seat opposite Raymie, arms dangling between her legs. Marcie reached out to pet Shainy. "How are you, pretty girl?"

she crooned. Shainy leaned her head closer so Marcie could scratch behind her ear.

Marcie looked over at Raymie, who could hear the excitement in her voice as she said, "Guess what?" Marcie leaned forward, pausing for effect: "We got a kitten! She's so cute! You and Shainy gotta come and see her!"

Raymie was washed over with uncertainty. Should she go to Marcie's house again so soon? But after meeting Marcie's excited gaze, Raymie gave in to the allure of a place that had felt so much like home.

Walking toward their house on the following Saturday, Raymie was cheered by the brilliant color of yellow and orange leaves on the tree that shaded their front yard. As she opened the gate, she saw what looked like a mound of something at one end of the yard. Curious, she moved closer to see a pile of leaves with a rake laid over the top in an effort, she supposed, to keep them from being scattered. She picked up one of the leaves that had escaped the pile and was fluttering about the ground. It felt light and papery in her hand. She lifted it to her nose to breathe in the pungent, mushroomy smell.

"They do smell wonderful, don't they?"

Raymie lifted her head. It was Jack, standing at the doorway, a light-colored bundle tucked into the crook of his arm, which Raymie imagined must be the new kitten.

"Come on in," Jack said, "Marcie had to fill in for a co-worker so she's running a little late. She should be here any minute, though."

Raymie followed him into the house, Shainy by her side. Shep appeared at the kitchen entryway and the two dogs greeted each other as old friends.

Jack gently set the kitten down on the kitchen floor and she skittered off to the next room. "I'll let Marcie introduce the kitten to you properly," Jack said. "I wouldn't want to spoil it for her." He stood a moment gazing in the direction the kitten had gone, then turned to Raymie, asking awkwardly, "Where do you want to be? I mean, is the kitchen okay while you wait?"

"The kitchen would be perfect," she told him. Raymie shrugged off her coat and placed it on the back of a chair, then went ahead and sat down, hoping by doing so she would put him more at ease. He seemed like a person who had a little trouble figuring out exactly what role he should take in a social situation. She liked that about him.

"Do you want some coffee?" he asked. "I just made it."

"Yes, please. It smells wonderful."

Jack poured them each a cup, said he'd wait with her and pulled up a chair.

Resting his elbows on the table to cradle the cup in his hands, Jack breathed in the aroma as the steam rose off his cup before taking the first sip.

Sitting across from him, Raymie suddenly became aware of everything about this man: the sleeves of his cotton shirt rolled to his elbows, the intake of his breath, his hands encircling the cup. Warmth spread through Raymie's body in pleasant shock. She took a sip of coffee to steady herself, surprised at the little prickle of sweat in her armpits, the slight tightening in her gut. Too aware of how close Jack was across the span of this small table, she leaned back in her chair as the heat moved to her cheeks, and calmed herself by reaching for Shainy beside her, head inclined to hide the blush behind the fringe of her hair while she ran her fingers over Shainy's soft fur.

"How long have you had Shainy?" Jack asked.

Raymie glanced up at him, grateful for the distraction of his question. "A little more than a year," she told him. "An agency in Oregon that trains guide dogs matched us up and then trained me, too, so that we could work together as a team." Raymie looked affectionately at Shainy. "It was a lot of work, but well worth it."

"I imagine it's a pretty comprehensive program, learning to work with guide dogs."

"I'll say!" Raymie grinned, shaking her head with the memory. "First there's an application and screening process. They can't just give anyone one of these dogs. Then once you're accepted to the program, you go through a two-week training course along with a group of other people. We joked about it being like boot camp, but, really, it was a lot more fun, especially when you get to meet your dog. That was the best part of all."

"So you don't get the dog right away?"

"No, we aren't paired with them until we've learned some primary handler skills. And even when you do meet your dog, it might not be the right match and so they try you with a different one. There was no problem with me and Shainy, though." Raymie smiled down at Shainy, who raised her head to meet Raymie's gaze. "It was love at first sight."

"You do seem like a good match. Shainy's a remarkable dog." Jack took a final sip, then set his cup down. Chin in hand, he asked, "I wonder how long guide dogs have been around. Do you know anything about their history? I'll bet they've been with us in some form or another for centuries."

"Oh, yes, they have quite a history," Raymie told him, hear-ing the eagerness in her own voice. "There's an ancient Roman mural that shows a dog leading a blind man, can you imagine that?"

"Wow. So, it certainly isn't a new idea."

"No, not by any means. There are records of people using guide dogs in Asia and Europe as early as the middle ages. No record of any special training method, though, until the late 1700's. That was in France, I think, or perhaps it was England. But the first real school started in Germany, during the first world war, when so many soldiers were blinded by exposure to mustard gas."

Jack nodded in a way that showed he was interested, but Raymie, afraid she was babbling, cautioned herself to slow down. "I could tell you more," she said, "but I really wouldn't want to bore you."

"Please do," he said, his voice tinged with humor.

"What?" Raymie said playfully, "Tell you more or bore you?"

He laughed and they sat there smiling at each other.

The dogs stood up, turned their heads toward the door, ears pricked.

Down the hallway was the sound of Marcie bursting through the door. Raymie turned her head toward the sound, a little disappointed that she would lose the time alone with Jack, but equally relieved, knowing that Marcie's presence would break the lingering tension she felt.

"Wow! It's getting cold out there, Jack!" Marcie announced. "Is Rainy here?"

Marcie spied Shainy, who had been released to go and greet her. "Oh, hi Shainy!" Raymie heard her say. "I guess Rainy is here!"

She walked into the kitchen, trailing Shainy and Shep. Raymie stood up and Marcie came over and hugged her. "Oops!" she said, covering her mouth. "I hope that's okay. Mom always told me to ask first before I go hugging people." Not waiting for Raymie's answer, she turned and hugged Jack, then stooped to pick up the kitten who had wandered into the kitchen, mewing for attention.

"So this," Marcie said, turning the kitten's face so Raymie could see her better, "is Sheba." She nuzzled the kitten's neck. "And you're a sweetie, aren't you?" She looked at Raymie, clearly pleased with herself. "And now we have Shep, Shainy and Sheba. Our little animal family."

Raymie heard Jack murmur, "I'm not sure if Raymie wants to include Shainy in—"

"Of course she does!" Marcie asserted.

The kitten rubbed her cheek against Marcie's hand, then gave it a little experimental bite.

"Ouch!" Marcie said loudly, then set the kitten down on the floor.

"That's how we teach her not to bite, right, Jack?"

"Right."

Marcie turned to Raymie. "Sheba's a good kitty, but she still has some things she has to learn. Jack and me are teaching her together."

"Jack and I," Jack muttered softly, his fondness for his sister-in-law apparent in his voice.

"Huh?" Marcie said, looking at Jack blankly.

"No big deal." He shook his head, smiling. "Never mind."

"You seem like a pretty good team to me," Raymie said, in an unnecessary attempt to smooth things over.

Marcie got herself a soda out of the refrigerator and she and Raymie decided to take the kitten outside to play in the leaves. (So much for the effort to keep them in a pile!) Jack sat on the top step in the weak October sunshine, sipping his coffee, the dogs lounging on either side of him. After a while he disappeared into the house.

"Probably talking to Cindy," Marcie said in a disgusted voice when Raymie noted his absence.

"Is that his girlfriend?"

"I guess," Marcie said, wrinkling her nose.

"You don't seem to like her very much."

Marcie shrugged. "I try."

"It must be hard seeing him with another person after all those years with your sister,"

"Oh, it's not that—I want Jack to be happy. It's just Cindy. She's just"—Marcie gave her head a little shake— "wrong."

Raymie had never seen Marcie like this, her eyes averted in distaste. She clearly didn't think that Cindy was a good match for Jack. Raymie caught herself thinking, 'So, who would be right for Jack?' followed by, 'You, Raymie? Is that what you're thinking? The Blind Lady? Oh, right. Great catch.'

Feeling the threat of angry tears at the back of her eyes, Raymie turned her attention to the kitten, who was cautiously stalking something at the base of the tree, jumping back, then moving slowly forward again. "Oh look, Marcie!" Raymie said, and using her most dramatic voice, told her, "Sheba the Adventure Cat has discovered something very menacing under the tree!"

Marcie giggled. "Oh! It's a big shiny beetle, Rainy!" Then joining in the game said, "Watch out, Sheba, that bug just might get you!"

Jack reappeared in time to help them scoop the leaves back in some semblance of a pile. "I've laid out some grapes and some crackers and cheese, in case you'd like something to munch on," he offered as he stuffed the leaves into the bag he'd brought out.

"That sounds marvelous," Raymie told him as she stood

up to brush leaves off her pants. "A person can certainly work up an appetite helping a fierce Adventure Cat track down a ferocious bug!" She glanced at Marcie, who burst into laughter. Jack gave an appreciative snort, head bent to his task, not giving eye contact. He's feeling just a little bit shy, Raymie thought, her heart warming to him in a way that was motherly, almost proprietary. Or maybe he just thinks I'm silly, came the next thought, making her shrink with embarrassment.

Jack tied off the bag and reached down to pick up Sheba. "Well now, you fearless Adventure Cat," he said playfully, "are you ready to go inside where it's warm?"

Raymie went into the house with Jack and Marcie, feeling accepted by the pair, happy in the thought that she had become part of the fold, that she somehow belonged there.

The three of them sat down to eat the snack, Marcie's chatter keeping Raymie relaxed and entertained. She noticed, not for the first time, how Marcie employed a mixture of seemingly naive audacity and a very sophisticated social sensitivity to set people at ease. As Marcie talked, drawing Raymie and Jack into conversation with one another, Raymie looked at her with admiration and wondered if very many people realized how skillful Marcie actually was. Successful social interaction is an art, and she had clearly mastered it, her style as offbeat as it was captivating.

The day was moving into late afternoon, the light outside beginning to fade. Raymie helped Marcie clear the table, then reaching for her coat on the back of the chair, said, "I'm afraid I have to get going now."

"Aw, can't you stay longer?" Marcie's voice was plaintive.

"That would be lovely," Raymie told her, "But I need to get home before dark."

Raymie had somehow twisted the sleeve of her coat and it wasn't going on smoothly, so uncharacteristic of her. Jack moved over to help with the sleeve, a little clumsy, Raymie thought, but sweet, the moment so quietly intimate that she had to suppress an urge to brush her cheek against his hand.

"I supposed you wouldn't accept a ride?" he said, the sound of his voice warm in her ear. Unable to speak, she shook her head, smiling her appreciation for the offer. "Well, it was good to see you," he told her. "I hope you come visit us again soon."

At that, Marcie looked up from where she was petting Shainy, "Jack!" she said excitedly, "Game night!"

Jack looked puzzled. "Yeah? That's still this coming Friday."

Marcie looked at him as if he were a bit of a dunce. "Game night, Jack," she slowly enunciated. "Let's invite Rainy to game night."

Jack looked at Raymie. "It's just a little family tradition," he offered hesitantly. "We spend one night a month playing board games. I don't know if you'd be interested."

"Sure she would!" Marcie insisted, sounding impatient with Jack.

"Actually," Raymie said slowly, "I do enjoy playing board games, if you wouldn't mind using modified versions, that is."

"Modified?" Marcie asked.

"Yes. Well, larger versions so that I can see the numbers and letters better. I could bring them here if you like."

"I'm sure that would work quite well," Jack said. "Don't you think so, Marcie?" She nodded her agreement, clutching Jack's arm in her mounting excitement.

"Well, good," Jack said, giving Marcie's hand at his elbow a little pat. "We'll see you Friday night." He paused, considering. "We usually start around seven. It would be dark by then. Can we come to pick you up?"

Raymie felt a sudden surge of happiness. "Oh, yes, I'd like that."

Jack smiled, then drew himself up, as if he'd just remembered something. He glanced at his watch. "Uh, sorry," he said, "I didn't realize the time. I have to be somewhere and I see I'm running way late."

Raymie heard Marcie emit a little sigh and thought, he's meeting his girlfriend. A picture formed in her mind of the woman Jack would choose: poised, talented and intelligent, and knew herself to be an outsider, her attraction to Jack an intrusion into this man's life. Raymie stepped back, and taking Shainy's leash in her hand, thanked them both for their hospitality.

"Are you sure you wouldn't at least like a ride to the bus stop?" Jack asked, sounding concerned.

"Oh no, it's just a few blocks. And I know you're in a hurry."

"I'll walk with you," Marcie said, going for her coat.

"Oh, thanks, Marcie, but I'll be fine on my own."

Raymie left the house quickly before either could protest further. She needed to be alone just then, to find solace in Shainy's quiet, steady company. Raymie had built a good enough life for herself since Bill's passing; She had her work and dance classes, a nice group of friends, her daughter and grandson close by. But this family, this family of two, Jack and Marcie, created a longing within her so visceral it hurt. Raymie knew with a deep certainty that she didn't want to be walking away from this house. She glanced behind her, the outlines of its facade already softened to a blur, and consoled herself with the thought that she would be returning there in less than a week.

20

Jack went to change his clothes while Marcie finished cleaning up from their visit with Raymie. She was nearly done when he came tearing past on his way to the door.

"Thanks for cleaning up, Marcie," he said, one hand busy buttoning his shirt cuff. One of the shirts Cindy gave him, Marcie saw, not his usual style. She shook her head.

"If you don't want to cook for yourself there are lots of leftovers in the fridge," he continued. "I probably won't be back until sometime in the morning."

"Okay," Marcie said, and closed the dishwasher door, maybe a little too hard.

As she heard the front door close, she thought, Cindy. Cripes, even her name made Marcie want to rub her nose, like there was a bad smell. She really had wanted to like Cindy for Jack's sake, even though she knew from the first time she met her that she wasn't right for him. At all. But the more she got to know Cindy, the more she disliked her. Cindy wasn't mean, especially, but she didn't seem to like good old Jack the way he was. She wanted him to be different, improved, and that was stupid. Marcie put the cracker box back in the cupboard and then jumped at the sound of herself slamming it shut. "Oops," she muttered.

Marcie frowned, remembering the day that she finally

threw up her hands and decided that no matter how she tried, she just wasn't going to like Cindy. Marcie had arrived home from work on an afternoon a couple of weeks ago to find Jack in the kitchen working at the stove. Noticing that there was a tablecloth on the table in the dining room, a room they rarely used, along with the good candlesticks and a small bouquet of flowers, she remembered that Jack had told her he was having Cindy over for dinner. Jeez, she hadn't thought it would be so fancy, though.

"Are you sure you don't want to join us for dinner?" he asked as he opened the lid to a pot.

"Wow, that smells really good Jack," she told him, breathing in the heady aroma of a mushroom sauce, "but you know, this is a special dinner for you and Cindy. I'm just gonna to put some on a plate and take it to my room."

The doorbell rang. Cindy entered, all shiny in perfect makeup, a low-cut blouse and jangly things on her wrist. Disgusting.

"Oh, hi Marcie," she said sweetly, and turned to Jack to give him a big kiss as though Marcie were not even in the room. "Oooo, something smells good!" she said when she had released him.

"I'll go ahead and fix myself a plate now," Marcie mumbled, but she stayed where she was sitting at the kitchen table.

Jack got a bottle of wine from the refrigerator, tilting it in invitation toward Marcie, who shook her head. Cindy, who was leaning against the counter gabbing away about something that happened at her job, gave Jack a nod and he poured a glass for her. As he was handing Cindy the glass his shirt sleeve got caught on the edge of the counter, who knows how, except that Jack had always been clumsy. His hand jerked and the wine flew forward, splashing all over Cindy's blouse. Marcie put her hand over her mouth to stifle a guffaw.

"Jesus, Jack," Cindy said, wiping frantically at her blouse with the dishtowel. "What are you, some kind of an idiot? Can't you at least try to be more careful?"

Jack didn't say anything. Marcie saw that he had this awful, 'Oh no, I did it again' kind of look on his face.

Marcie's mirth suddenly turned to anger. Before she could think whether it was a good idea or not, she turned to Cindy, outrage in her voice. "He does try, Cindy! Give him a break! It just happens sometimes!"

Cindy's head swiveled toward Marcie, her eyes squeezed and her mouth in a tight little line, looking like she wanted her to just die, so Marcie stared right back until Cindy dropped her eyes and turned away to look at Jack. "Oh well, no harm done," she said in a sticky sweet voice.

Marcie got up and left the room. Fuming, she got her wallet out of her bedroom and put on her coat. There was a Subway about a half-mile away. She'd get herself a sandwich.

When she got to the Subway, she saw that her friend from Special Olympics, Brandon, was working that day. "Hi Marcie," he said, as he wiped down a table. "How're you doing today?"

"Fine," Marcie answered, sounding grumpy.

"Hang on Marcie, I'm gonna ask my boss if I can take a break. You don't look so happy."

Marcie got her sandwich and Brandon came and sat across from her, sucking up the large soda he'd poured himself.

"I thought your mom didn't want you to drink soda anymore."

Brandon shrugged. "What's up with you Marcie? Something bad happen?"

Marcie explained about the incident with Cindy between angry bites of a meatball sandwich messy with tomato sauce. Brandon gave his soda a thoughtful slurp. "I don't get it about you and Cindy, Marcie, because you seem to like everybody no matter what."

"I know, but she's so different from how my sister Lisa was, and I just can't understand what Jack sees in her."

She paused and Brandon gave her a sage nod, which helped Marcie calm down a little. "I think I'd like Cindy okay fine if I knew her from somewhere else, you know, like not Jack's girlfriend, but she plain old doesn't fit with Jack. Doesn't she know that? Doesn't he know that?"

Brandon just sat there looking at her, possibly preparing to say something wise. "You got meatball sauce on your face," he told her.

Marcie laughed, wiping the sauce off her chin. Okay, so maybe she was taking this whole thing a little too seriously.

21

Both hands gripping the steering wheel, Jack consciously slowed his breathing as he took a left toward the highway. He was late, but so what? Cindy wasn't exactly known for punctuality herself. His tension returned as he remembered that she had a real double standard about that, and heaven forbid the person who would keep her waiting. And today she would be especially upset because they were going to some grandiose store opening for her work. She had prodded him until he said yes, but he didn't really want to go. He didn't have much in common with her co-workers and disliked having to make idle chitchat and to be expected to laugh at an insider's merchandising joke that he didn't really understand.

He accelerated well above the speed limit on the highway, then made himself ease off on the pedal and relax back into his seat. He turned off into a section of town populated by clusters of townhouses and apartments all competing for the best view from their upper stories. Driving past a row of near-identical apartment buildings he heard himself mutter, "What the hell are you doing here, Jack?" He looked up, located Cindy's balcony among a beehive of others just like it and added, "This isn't your world."

This was no great revelation. Thinking back to how he got involved with Cindy he often experienced the same bewilderment.

The evening he'd met her he'd gone to a party at the home of his colleague Joyce and her husband Robert. Lisa had been gone more than three years by then, and people had started earnestly pushing women at him, women who were quite suitable candidates: smart, well-read, independent and attractive, very much like Lisa, minus her wild streak. But he had resisted their attempts, not ready to replace Lisa with someone new.

He'd just accepted a glass of wine from Joyce when Robert answered the door and started to introduce his niece to the other guests. "And this is Jack," he was saying as he led the niece toward him, "the one who works with Joyce."

"Hi Jack," she said, offering him her fingertips to shake, and Jack thought, "Oh, right, they've told her about me, the single guy, the guy who lost his wife."

She lingered, standing close to Jack as she chatted with Robert about the recent trip he and Joyce had taken to Baja. As she talked Jack took a moment to assess her, almost amused at himself for doing so. Cindy was pretty, a little too done up for his taste, heavily but precisely made up, her hair dyed a blonde that seemed too young for her age, which he figured to be late forties or early fifties. She was wearing stilettos, which Lisa always condemned as the worst possible things for a woman's feet, but on Cindy were actually quite attractive. Nice legs, he found himself thinking, surprised because he normally didn't think that way. But he sensed that she wanted him to think 'nice legs,' so he did.

Robert left to get Cindy a glass of wine, leaving the two of them alone. "So, Jack," Cindy said, leaning to the side to brush his shoulder lightly with hers, "how long have you been teaching?"

Jack took a sip of his wine, "It's been about thirty years now, give or take a few. I taught high school classes before I moved on to college."

"Joyce says you're the best in the department."

Jack tucked in his chin. "Oh, I wouldn't say that. Joyce underestimates her own abilities. She's very good, especially with the freshmen classes. Those can be excruciating for the students if they don't have the right teacher."

"Uh huh," Cindy said, eyes on the rest of the people in the crowded room. Robert appeared briefly at her side, a glass of wine proffered to Cindy before moving off to deliver a beer to another guest. Cindy thanked him before turning to Jack to say, "I'm in merchandising. That is, I'm a buyer for a clothing store." She swirled the wine in her glass, tasted it, nodded her approval. "The store's a good one, pretty high-end, 'The Smart Lady'. Have you heard of it?"

Jack shook his head and she continued: "It's a companion store to 'The Smart Gentleman' which is just across from it in the mall."

Jack, who generally avoided the mall, had never heard of either.

"It's a good job, but I can do better," she was telling him. "I'm currently looking for a position with Nordstrom's. It's hard to get on with them, but I think I have a shot."

They were joined by Joyce just then, who hugged Cindy warmly but carefully. Jack made a guess that Cindy had taught the exuberant Joyce not to smudge her makeup.

"The buffet's ready," Joyce told them. "You two grab some plates."

Moving to the buffet table together, they filled their plates and found seats side by side on the couch. "Try this," Cindy said. She leaned close to put some pasta salad on his plate. "It's Robert's specialty." Jack, who got a glimpse of her small rounded breasts before he averted his eyes, felt a flicker of desire.

He tried a bite.

"Good, hmm?" Cindy said, coquettishly dabbing at his mouth with her napkin.

Jack rolled his eyes in exaggerated appreciation and she gave a short laugh, smiling at him.

He watched Cindy as she bent over her own plate and realized that she would probably go home with him if he asked. Jack knew he wouldn't ask. He missed sex, but didn't know how to approach it with a new person. He didn't even think he had a condom, which he was pretty sure was a requirement for casual sex these days.

By the end of the evening Cindy asked to exchange phone numbers.

She called him the next day.

He wouldn't call her voice sensual, its tempo was more staccato than smooth, but there was a seductive quality that brought to mind a panther circling its prey, and Jack responded with self-protective caution. He suggested a café near the college where they could have lunch during the two hours set aside for his lunch break and planning period, followed by a walk on a nearby bike path. The time limit imposed by having to return to work would eliminate, he hoped, the possibility of her pouncing on him before he was ready.

Cindy met him at the café, a little late but unapologetic. He noticed right away, that despite her too-tight jeans paired with high heels—definitely a combination meant to give a certain message—she had put the brakes on her seductive approach. He smiled with satisfaction as he watched her open the menu; the daytime date had been the right way to go. They both ordered the special, Cindy launching into an easy rambling dialog, seemingly about whatever came to mind. She continued through the meal, mostly talking about herself with occasional questions about Jack's life, the answers to which seemed only to segue back into further talk about herself. She was easy to listen to and required little from him other than a nod or an "Is that so?" now and again.

When they had finished their lunch, Cindy pushed her chair back from the table and declared, "If we're taking a walk we'll need to go to my car to get my jogging shoes," and had him follow her to an immaculate newer model Lexus. "Nice car," he told her, although it was a far cry from the decades-old Volvo that Lisa used to drive, a car he truly loved, its oxidized blue paint making it look soft and welcoming. He smiled at the memory. It was never all that clean and there was always a pile of stuff crammed in the back end.

Cindy's voice pulled him away from the memory. "You like it?" she said, glancing up at him as she tied her shoe. "A friend of mine works at a dealership and this came in on a trade. I got a good deal, but it's still kind of a stretch. Worth it, though, for the impression it makes, don't you think?"

"It does seem to make an impression," Jack said, wondering who she wanted to impress.

Cindy was a vigorous walker, which suited Jack, and as soon as they were on the path she resumed her monologue. What she spoke of lacked in depth, allowing Jack to split his attention between her and a particularly poignant bird song, the sound of children playing, the bicycles whizzing by. He didn't mind the way she monopolized the conversation: there wasn't much he wanted to say to her and Cindy seemed so comfortable in her own skin that it made him feel relaxed, realizing that this kind of easy companionship was exactly what he needed at this time of his life. When the path looped back to the parking lot near the café, he noted the time and walked with her to her car. She stood waiting for him to open the car door, which he appreciated because he was never sure what was expected of him in that quarter. Holding the door open, he leaned over to give her a quick kiss on the cheek.

"That was fun, Jack. We should get together again soon," she told him as she slid into the seat.

What the heck, Jack thought. He may as well. "How about dinner this weekend?" he asked her. "I'm free either day—what about you?"

That Saturday they drove together to a Mediterranean restaurant in Seattle. After they were seated, Cindy put on a pair of reading glasses to scan the menu, careful to take them off before she looked up at Jack. "I have an idea," she said, scooting her chair a little closer to his, "Let's each order something we've never had before and then share bites. What do you think?"

"Sure, why not? That would be fun," Jack said. "What sounds interesting to you? I've only had spanakopita, the spinach pie, once, and that was years ago. I'd like to try it again."

"Never heard of it," she said with a shrug. "Let's order it. I'm always willing to try something new."

They went to her apartment, after the usual euphemistic invitation to go up for a drink, and Jack was happy that he'd bought condoms the day before.

In bed Cindy was skillful in a studied way, there was no

sense of abandon like he'd had with Lisa, but he felt thrilled with her and himself, realizing just how much he'd missed the act of making love.

When they finally rolled apart, satiated, he lay next to her in bed, his hand running the length of her curved leg while she talked about a movie she had watched about warring fashion designers. He listened, made appropriate comments, feeling drowsy and happy, noticing how nice it was to share a bed with someone again, how good it felt not to be alone.

In the months that followed Jack got into the habit of reminding himself what it was that he liked about Cindy. For example, though always very careful to project the sophisticate around Jack's friends and her co-workers, she could be spontaneous and playful when they were alone together, prone to pillow fights and coming up with new, silly or bawdy lyrics to a well-known song. One time she impulsively made him pull into a playground on their way home from a movie so that she could swing on the swing set. Her whoops of joy echoed through the empty playground as, leaning back in the seat, she pumped her legs high into the air, her skirt flying behind her. For a moment she seemed like the child she must once have been, and he found himself smiling fondly.

When they got back into the car, she threw her arms around his neck and declared, "I love you, Jack Wallace!"

There was a heartbeat of hesitation before Jack told her he felt the same. He did, didn't he?

Jack maneuvered into the covered parking area outside Cindy's apartment wondering again why he chose Cindy out of all the women he'd been introduced to. Was it because she was so completely unlike Lisa? Her body type, her coloring, her ideology were nothing like the woman he'd loved for more than twenty-six years. It made so little sense that it made sense. She distracted him from the grief that had paralyzed him for so long. A part of him felt that this was unfair to Cindy, but the little tug of guilt he felt wasn't enough to make him change course.

Emerging from the car, he took a moment to re-tuck his shirt and brush a hand over the front of his blazer, the best one he had, but he noticed it was getting a little seedy. He shrugged and walked up a flight of exterior stairs to the door of her apartment.

"You're late!" Cindy told him as soon as she opened the door.

"Yeah, sorry. Marcie had a friend over and I lost track of time."

"You spend way too much time entertaining Marcie and her little friends," Cindy said, then seeming to think that was too harsh, added, "That's very nice of you Jack, but it shouldn't interfere with our time together."

Jack stood at the doorway, silent a moment as it finally sunk in that Cindy and Marcie didn't like each other, and probably never would.

Cindy gave a little impatient huff and he stepped into her apartment, noting again how antiseptically clean it was, to the point of being almost devoid of personality. "We have to go soon," she told Jack, "but first, look! I bought you something," she said, handing him a shopping bag sporting a logo of a man in a bowler hat.

"What's this?" Jack said, looking suspiciously at the bag.

"The Smart Gentleman was having a sale and I picked up a little something that's going to be perfect for you." She took the bag from him and pulled out a well-tailored blazer. "Here," she said removing the tags, "try it on." Jack tried on the jacket, which was a surprisingly good fit and had an expensive feel to the fabric. Cindy stepped back, appraising his appearance. "That looks fabulous on you," she said, "and the jeans you're wearing are kind of sexy with it." She paused, frowning. "But those shoes are all wrong. We'll find you a better pair later." Jack's mood quickly changed to annoyance. He opened his mouth to protest, then decided to let it go.

His annoyance returned when they got to the store opening and Cindy introduced him to her new supervisor as Dr. Wallace. It wasn't that he minded the recognition for his PhD, but he felt like she was showing him off to this man, someone she clearly wanted to impress. "Just Jack is fine," he assured him after Cindy, oblivious to his discomfort, left him alone with the new supervisor to make some kind of polite small talk until the time the guy could find someone more interesting to talk to and Jack could wander over to the refreshments table.

That night, getting ready for bed at her apartment, Jack said, "Listen, Cindy, I don't want you making me out to be more than I am."

Fingers busy taking off an earring, she said, "What do you mean by that?"

"I mean, let's drop this Dr. Wallace stuff. I teach community college. A few of my students call me Dr. Wallace, but mostly it's Mr. Wallace or even Jack, and that's how I like it. I only got the damn PhD because the dean was pressuring me to do it."

"Well Jack, don't you think it's time to get the recognition you deserve?" Cindy said, kicking off her heels and padding across the rug toward the bathroom. "And why stop at community college? Why not teach at a university where you'd make a lot more money?" She stood in front of the mirror, wiping off her makeup. "Time to think big, Jack. Why limit yourself?"

They went to bed. After a brief episode of lackluster sex, Jack lay with his hands behind his head looking into the dark, thinking that this poorly built edifice they had hammered together, their relationship, was starting to sag and crack at the seams.

Well, what did you think? Jack asked himself as he examined the cracks, the crumbling foundation. Didn't you realize this relationship would be temporary, a place to be while you recovered from what you lost? Immediately Jack felt guilt at his disloyalty to Cindy. He turned on his side to curve his body around her sleeping form, trying once again to convince himself that he loved her.

22

THE OUTFIT she'd worn to dance class in a satchel slung over her shoulder, Raymie unlocked the door to the 1940's bungalow that she and Bill had bought when Allison was still in grade school, grateful as always for the comfortable serenity of its arched doorways and worn wood floors. Breathing in the scent of home, she tucked the bundle of dance clothes into the laundry basket, fed Shainy and went to shower in preparation for her evening at Marcie and Jack's house, all the while trying to ignore the little twinge of nerves she felt. After all, it was just a casual get-together, a family game night, she told herself, as she checked the temperature of the water.

Wet hair wrapped in a towel and wearing her old terry cloth robe over skin damp from the shower, Raymie went to the closet to choose something to wear. Opening the closet door, she smiled when she saw how neatly Ellen, a wonderful woman she'd hired through a caregiving service, had organized the closet by type and color. Raymie felt so lucky to have found Ellen. She had no prior experience with a person who was blind but was open to learning about Raymie's world and wonderfully tolerant of the occasional meltdowns Raymie would have, frustrated with trying to do something that was easy a year or two ago and was now nearly beyond her reach as her sight deteriorated.

Ellen came once a week to take Raymie grocery shopping, go over the spots she'd missed while cleaning and to do things like arrange the condiments in her refrigerator so that Raymie could tell one from the other and be fairly certain, for example, that she was about to open the mustard, not the jam.

Raymie's kitchen had been modified so that she could still do some cooking. There was a full-spectrum florescent light installed under one of the cabinets, along with her latest addition, a mounted magnifier. She had always loved to make salads, and by using the intense light and magnifier to check the vegetables for blemish or rot, she was still able to do that. As she looked through her blouses, she found herself thinking about the strawberries she'd bought to take to this evening's get-together. She had picked them up at the supermarket on the way home from class and before Jack and Marcie came to pick her up, she planned to look at them under the bright light to get a better sense of their condition.

She remembered the day Bill had installed that light for her. It was around two or three years before he had died.

"Do you really think you need this, Raymie?" he asked as he screwed the case into the bottom of the cabinet.

Standing in the doorway watching him work, Raymie couldn't believe he'd said that. How could he not know how hard this was for her, how she struggled to do everyday tasks?

"Well, Bill, you've complained about potato peels ending up in the stew. This will help me avoid that."

"Listen, I don't mean to make you feel bad, Raymie, but don't you think you're exaggerating this vision problem a little bit? I mean, everybody's like, poor little Raymie, is there anything we can do for you? It would be hard not to want the attention."

Raymie closed her eyes and leaned her head against the doorframe, feeling weary. Bill had such a talent for negativity. He looked up from his work, saw her defeated expression. "Okay, sorry, Raymie," he said, his tone edging toward contempt. "I just wanted to check that out with you. I wasn't trying to say anything negative so don't go into that poor me bit again, okay."

Poor me bit? Raymie wasn't aware of any poor me bit she did, at least no more than other people. She thought that she was projecting a fairly stoic attitude about her vision loss.

Shaking off her bewilderment, she reminded herself that Bill was probably even more irritable than usual because he had been so sick lately. But did that excuse all the times over the years he had criticized and belittle her? She was so tired of it.

"It's okay, Bill," she told him, careful to conceal the weariness in her voice. "Thanks for installing the light."

Standing at her open closet Raymie shook her head to clear off the memory and consciously searched for a better one, a memory of a time when she and Bill were happy together. She sifted through her clothes, trying to find just the right outfit for that evening. Her fingers brushed against the fabric of a blouse that Bill had bought for her. Raymie had loved that blouse. So long that it was nearly a dress, it was black with pale blue embroidery, probably an import from India, though the label gave no hint. It cinched in at her waist and billowed out around her hips. Taking it off the clothes rack, Raymie held it to her body, moving it back and forth to swish about her thighs. Bill had bought it on impulse for no reason, he said, other than that he loved her, which made Raymie so happy that she proposed they drop the chores they'd planned to go on a picnic together. Allie was at her father's for the day, so Bill and Raymie bought a bottle of wine and a variety of delicacies to eat and headed for a waterfront park.

He'd taken a picture of Raymie that day at the park, sitting on the picnic blanket under a tree, laughing at some crack he'd made. Squinting in the too-bright sun, a bloom of summer freckles sprinkled across her cheeks, her face was filled with joy.

Fingering the embroidery on the sleeve, Raymie remembered how they tossed everything from the picnic on the couch when they got home and went straight to the bedroom, making love with the blouse still on, laughing at the depth of their own urgency. Afterward he didn't pull away as he often did but nuzzled up against Raymie's neck. Raymie lay there with her cheek resting on the top of his head, glowing with happiness, gently stroking his back, watching as the last bright light of the fading day trickled through a part in the curtain and flickered against the wall: dark, light, dark, light.

The doorbell woke them both. "Oh no, Bill, it's Don bringing Allie home!" Raymie said as she pulled on her jeans. She heard Ron say through the door, "Raymie?"

"Be there in a minute," she called as she hurried to the door, hooking her bra and fastening her buttons as she went, Bill padding behind her in bare feet, looking wonderfully goofy, Raymie thought, with his shirt half-tucked. Before they opened the door with their enthusiastic greetings for the returning Allison, Bill and Raymie looked at each other, faces flushed with sleep and sex, and laughed softly like two children who had shared a secret adventure.

Head tilted to one side, Raymie smiled at the memory. She still missed Bill sometimes. Not the bad times, sure, but those rare moments of sweetness when she could see the boy he once was before something within him turned sour.

Raymie put the blouse back on the rack. It was definitely not the one she would wear that evening.

23

OLYMPIA, WASHINGTON, 1983

RAYMIE LOOKED AT the heading of her paper. Another error. No, two! She pulled the piece of paper out of the typewriter, wadded it into a ball and dropped it into the wastebasket. Sighing, she rubbed her eyes, which seemed to be giving her more trouble than ever these days, remembering too late that she was wearing her contacts. She blinked. Oh good, they didn't get dislodged. Raymie looked at the notes strewn across the table. She was glad to be back in school again but it was exhausting running from class to work, to Allison's daycare, then trying to fit in homework whenever and wherever she could. And was she being a bad mother? The underlying anxiety she felt about spending too much time away from Allison coupled with the stress of school was sometimes just too much. She reminded herself, as she often did, that she only needed to do this one year to complete the degree she'd barely missed getting six years earlier. Raymie arched her back to stretch out her tight muscles. She felt like she needed a break, something fun, but knew she'd probably just have to settle for some chocolate. Did she have some in the kitchen?

She was just getting up from her chair when the phone rang.

"Hi Raymie! This is Janice. From your ethics class?"

"Oh yes! How are you?"

"Oh, I'm doing fine, considering that I'm buried in homework."

"I hear you there."

"It's the pits, all right. But listen, remember how at lunch the other day we were talking about how much we both love to dance? It just so happens my friend Jill and I are going dancing on Saturday, want to come with us?"

"Oh, Janice! That sounds like fun! I haven't been dancing for ages. Are you thinking about going to a place here in Olympia?"

"No, I was actually thinking about Seattle. That's where the best music is. I like punk and new-wave, and of course, there's always classic rock, but that's usually an older crowd."

"Punk is interesting, but body slamming isn't my idea of dancing. How about a new-wave band? Let me see if Mom can take Allison for the night, and then, yes, let's go dancing!"

"Oh, that's right, you have a daughter. How old is she?"

"She just turned five."

"I'll bet she's cute. You get along okay with her dad?"

"Don and I are on fairly good terms, but I wish he'd spend more time with Allie. He's not in her life a whole lot now that he's remarried, but he does see her every couple of weeks and he sends child support religiously."

"Huh. What happened with you two? I want to know because Peter and I are talking about getting married next year."

"That's wonderful news about you and Peter!" Raymie paused. "Can you hang on a minute Janice?" She set the receiver on the table and went to check on Allison, who was playing quietly in her room. She picked up the phone again. "Okay. I just wanted to make sure Allie was out of hearing range. She loves her dad, and he's not a bad guy."

"So, why'd you two split up?"

"Oh, gee, where do I start? I met him during my wild days at PLU. I was the stereotypical minister's daughter, you know, who got a little too crazy as soon as I got away from my parents' control."

"PLU? Isn't that a Christian college?"

'Yes, it is, but we were still your normal college kids with our first experience of being away from home."

"I know how that is," Janice said. "You should have seen me in my freshman year. That was one long party. I'm surprised I didn't flunk out. So, you were pretty wild, huh? Lots of guys?"

"Well, I wasn't exactly a nymphomaniac, but I indulged in what I like to describe as rapid-fire serial monogamy." Raymie heard Janice chuckle knowingly. "None of them were serious relationships," she continued, "and they didn't last very long. Don was just like the others, except that I got pregnant. He begged me to marry him, and my parents were all for it, so I married a man I didn't really love, quit school in my senior year, no less, and had my beautiful daughter. I guess you can fill in the rest."

"So, you guys didn't work out as a couple?"

"That's right, we just weren't a very good fit. But listen, it sounds like you and your boyfriend really want to be together and that's a very different story." Raymie assured her, "You should be just fine."

They made plans for Saturday and Janice said goodbye, only to call back a few minutes later. "I forgot to tell you," Janice said. "I told Jill that you were a really good dancer, almost professional, and she wanted me to tell you that you should audition for this community theater play she's in."

"Oh dear. It sounds tempting, but I can't imagine fitting something more into my schedule."

"Jill's dance instructor told her that you can get credit for it as an independent study class."

"Hmm. Okay, I'll talk to her about it on Saturday."

"She says the director is pretty good. His name is Bill something or other."

Raymie didn't consider herself much of an actor, but the play, a musical production of A Midsummer Night's Dream, gave her an opportunity to dance onstage and it held the additional allure of college credits. It was just a small part, she reasoned, and wouldn't take all that much extra time. She decided that she may as well go to the audition.

Janice offered to watch Allison while Raymie auditioned. Waiting her turn backstage in the dim theater, Raymie tried to calm her nerves, telling herself that it didn't really matter whether she got the part or not. When her name was called, she hesitated a few seconds while she steadied her breath, then walked onto the empty stage. She spoke a few lines, her voice quavering, and danced woodenly, she thought. Bill, the director, didn't seem very impressed. She went home, relieved that it was over.

She was surprised when Bill called her back for a second audition. Not able to find a sitter at short notice, she brought Allison with her and settled her into one of the theater seats with some toys.

Raymie felt frail and exposed up there on the stage. Bill, standing below in the pit, appeared so large, a handsome bulldog of a man, with a wide jaw and chest. He had his head down and was writing as she walked in. Looking up, he pointed his pen at her. "So why do you want to be a part of this production? Have you done Shakespeare before?"

"Well, no, I've taken a Shakespeare class and read his plays aloud, and I know that I really enjoy them, but no. I just really love to dance and this part is mostly dancing. That's why I'm here. To dance."

"Oh. To dance. And you think there's nothing to the speaking part of the role?"

Raymie shifted her shoulders, unconsciously smoothing the front of her dress. Damn! She promised herself she wouldn't do that! "Oh no, I think that the speaking part is very important."

He just looked at her. Waiting.

"I promise I'll do the best I can with it."

"The best you can?" He gave a snort of derision, turned his head, and looked at the clipboard he was holding.

After a moment she said, "Well, it was nice to meet you."

He snorted again, then said, "Rehearsals start on Thursday at seven. Don't be late."

Raymie's impression of Bill as an arrogant, pretentious jerk never did completely alter, but her heart opened to the ways that he was vulnerable, and even needy. She eventually decided that the arrogance was only partly real, and was as much a protective front as anything else.

He called her "tiny dancer" because she was so small. It might have been construed as demeaning, but Raymie could hear the fondness attached to it. After a while, it held the soft coo of love, and when he touched her to adjust her position on stage, she could feel the jolt of attraction. When he suggested that they go for a beer after rehearsal one evening, she was ready. By opening night, they were holding hands, clearly in love.

Bill stopped directing community theatre as his newspaper

job ramped up, and Raymie never auditioned for another part, but what they'd begun continued beyond the sweat and glitter of the theater, seeing each other several times a week.

It was an evening in early November. The weather had turned cool, but the soft sheen of streetlights on the wet pavement cheered her as Raymie and Bill walked side by side down the sidewalk on their third date, dinner at a Vietnamese restaurant followed by a film festival. It had been a wonderful evening; the dinner was perfect and they both had loved the film.

As they turned the corner toward his car, it seemed like the natural thing for Raymie to reach for Bill's hand. He held it loosely, seeming uncomfortable with the closeness it represented.

After a few moments he gave her hand a little squeeze and dropped it before turning to her.

"Listen, Raymie," he told her, "there's something I need to talk to you about." He shoved his hands deep into his pockets as he plunged forward, his pace increasing, shoulders hunched, head down. Raymie quicken her steps to keep up, trying to get a glimpse of his face.

"You see, Raymie," he told her, "you poor unsuspecting fool, you've been dating a guy who is a brittle diabetic." He gave her a rough glance as he slowed his pace. "I didn't realize I had it until about six years ago. I should have known something was up, because I'd been having these problems since I was a kid, but after I started college was when it got really bad. I was gaining weight for no reason, you know? When I would try to cut back on food, I'd get kind of frantic to eat, like I had to consume everything in sight. It was so weird. I finally went to the doctor to find out what was going on and he told me I was a diabetic. I couldn't believe I had diabetes. At 22." He shook his head. "I'd always thought that was an old man's disease. And the kind I have, well, it's the worst kind, and it's practically a death sentence." He stopped and turned to look at her. "Anyway, what I'm trying to tell you, Raymie, is that I'm probably not going to live to old age. I have to take insulin every day." Bill took a ragged breath. "It pisses me off, but this is my life." He stopped and put his hands on her shoulders, his gaze direct, challenging. "I thought you should know about this before we get any more serious about each other. If you want to back out I'd understand."

Raymie looked into Bill's eyes, surprised to hear that he was battling a chronic illness. He seemed so bold and confident, so robust; how could he have a life-threatening disease? It really couldn't be as bad as he described, could it? It only took her a moment to make a decision. "I'm not the kind of person who abandons someone because they're sick, Bill," she told him, placing a hand on his cheek. "Whatever this means for you, I will be there."

He hooked his arm through hers. "Okay, as long as you know what you're getting into."

They continued to see each other, Bill no longer hiding the insulin kit that he kept in his bathroom cabinet.

After they had been dating more than a year a small collection of Bill's clothing had accumulated in Raymie's closet, and Allison's toys were frequently strewn across Bill's living room. On a Sunday in November, Raymie was at Bill's place, getting ready to head home so that Allison could be ready for school the next day. The zipper on Allison's coat had stuck, and Raymie was bending over her daughter yanking on the pull when Bill spoke behind her. "Don't you think it's a little stupid, this running back and forth between our two apartments?"

"Well, yes, Bill, but Allison's school clothes are at home. We can come back in a few days."

"Why not just stay here all the time? It would be a lot less hassle, and if we lived together it'd be cheaper for both of us."

Raymie twisted to look at him, hands still on Allison's coat. Allison had started to squirm, and Raymie was getting exasperated with the zipper. "You mean live here, Bill? What about your roommate?"

"Blake got a gig with a paper in Tacoma. He's leaving at the end of the month."

Finally getting the zipper to move, Raymie finished pulling it to Allison's chin before she turned. "So, you want me to be your new roommate? Because it would be less of a hassle and everybody would save money?"

"Well, Raymie, do you think it might have something to do with the fact that I love you?" This was said teasingly, with a small smirk.

But he had said he loved her. At last. "I love you too, Bill," she said softly. "I'm sure you know that."

"So why don't you and Allison move in here?"

"Oh, but Bill, my dad would be furious. You know how he feels about unmarried couples living together."

"So, you're still letting yourself be run by your old man? Mr. holier-than-thou Reverend Ray Jamieson."

"I thought you liked him."

"Yeah, well, he's okay. You just shouldn't let him run your life. Time to act like a big girl, Raymie."

Hoping her parents would eventually accept her decision to live with Bill, Raymie took him up on his invitation to share his apartment. Raymie's mother seemed okay with the move, but Ray Jamieson, as predicted, was incensed. He refused to have anything to do with his daughter, imperiously proclaiming, "She's not allowed here until she wises up and does the right thing."

After months of isolation from her family, Raymie finally gave in and told Bill that she was going to look for another place for her and Allison. Bill, watching her look through the newspaper ads for housing, said, "What the hell, Raymie, we may as well get married."

"Are you sure, Bill?" Raymie said, lowering the newspaper to look at him. He had told her on several occasions that he thought marriage was a trap that he planned to avoid at all costs.

"Why not?" he said with a shrug, "It's what people do, isn't it? Let's just hope it turns out better than my folks' marriage."

Regarding him with surprise, Raymie saw just the crinkle of a smile at the corner of Bill's eyes, a smile of happiness. She wondered if he had been thinking about this all along and had just needed an excuse to recant what he had said about marriage.

The wedding was at Raymie's father's church, at his insistence, even though the couple would have preferred a non-religious setting.

It was a fairly small affair. One of Bill's brothers attended, but Bill hadn't invited either of his parents. Raymie had never met his father, who by Bill's account, was a swaggering, bombastic self-made man who abandoned Bill's mother and their three boys to live in poverty while he went on expensive vacations with his new wife.

Raymie had urged Bill to invite his mother, whom she had

met briefly when Sherrie visited Bill back when he and Raymie were first dating. Raymie had taken an instant liking to Sherrie, who was a sweet, kindhearted woman, and would have loved for her to come, but Bill had said he was sure she was too busy with her life in Wyoming to travel all the way to Washington state. Raymie suspected that it was more than that. From what she'd gathered, Sherrie had become very depressed after the divorce, slipping into alcoholism. From the time he was twelve years old until he left for college, Bill took care of the house and his two younger brothers. Suffocated by her neediness, Bill had to fight his way free of his mother's dependence in order to have a life of his own. As an adult, he was kind to his mother, but wouldn't allow her into his life.

Raymie decided it was a nice wedding despite Bill's apparent lack of interest. Raymie's family and several of her friends came, and Allie stole the show as the flower girl.

After the ceremony there was a brief reception and then they got in the car to drive to Portland for the weekend while Allison stayed with Raymie's parents.

Traveling south down I5, Bill silent beside her, Raymie wrapped herself in the happiness of the occasion. "It was so good that Brice and Emily could come. And your brother traveled such a long way. Wasn't it just wonderful to see him?"

Bill, eyes on the road, in a voice devoid of any enthusiasm, said, "Yeah, I was glad he could make it."

Raymie tried a different tact. "And wasn't Allison just so cute? I loved how everyone reacted when she came down the aisle with her little basket of rose petals. I'm glad my aunt put that together for her—she did a nice job, don't you think?"

Bill was silent, only giving a short nod. Raymie, her buoyancy waning, slumped in her seat. Arms crossed across her chest for comfort, she looked out the window, fighting back tears.

A few moments later Bill turned his head toward her. "Well, you got your way, didn't you, Raymie? Just what you wanted." She looked at him, her mouth open but unable to speak as he added, "A nice little wedding to keep mommy and daddy happy."

Raymie rolled down the window to cool the flush on her face. How could he say that? His eyes had been soft with love as they exchanged vows and afterward, as the guests crowded toward them, he threw an arm, in a way that seemed casual, around her shoulders, but she could feel the tremble in his body and the swell of his chest as he accepted the congratulations.

Bill wasn't going to admit how happy he was to be married to her. But what had she expected? With Bill, this was as good as it gets. It was almost as if he didn't trust happiness. As if to acknowledge it was to banish it.

The early years of their marriage were good. At least, good enough. Bill was a popular man. There were often invitations from friends at the paper where he worked, and even though he was no longer involved in community theater, he and Raymie were invited to play openings and cast parties. There were plenty of family outings too. Bill seemed to adore Allison and the three of them went to museums, movies and the beach.

Their lives together took a new turn when Bill landed a good job with a bigger paper. They moved to a nice two-bedroom bungalow outside of Poulsbo, in a neighborhood where there were families with children Allison's age. Shortly after that Raymie began the arduous process of putting herself through graduate school, making the long commute to her college and working part-time, minimum wage jobs.

It was during this time that Bill became increasingly dismissive of things Raymie found important. He was often sarcastic with her, and would withdraw into angry silences, especially when she approached any subject that he found distasteful or uncomfortable, including pleas for him to help more around the house so that she could do homework.

Raymie completed graduate school and began her career as a speech therapist. She achieved a good reputation in her profession, but Bill didn't seem impressed by her accomplishments.

By his early forties, the debilitating symptoms of Bill's Type I diabetes, which he had managed to keep at bay for so long, made themselves known. He had hoped to be one of the exceptions; but it became apparent that he wasn't going to escape the prognosis he was given when first diagnosed: that he could expect an early death.

As the disease progressed, he became bitter and angry. Already a proud, thin-skinned man who like to have control over every situation, these qualities grew stronger as his very essence of being was challenged. Always a bit of a drinker, he turned to alcohol to assuage his frustration and pain.

24

IT WAS A MONDAY EVENING a few days after the lackluster event that was their eleventh anniversary. Raymie returned from work to find Bill sitting in front of the television, glass in hand, his stockinged feet propped up on the coffee table next to a half-finished bottle of bourbon. From its lurid label she could see that it was the cheap stuff, not the expensive brand that he liked to sip for pleasure.

She put her briefcase in the closet and took off her coat. In the living room, she saw Bill's shoes in a pile and his coat thrown over a chair. A glance into the adjoining dining room told her that the greasy smell that permeated the house came from a crumpled fast food bag sitting on the table, an open bottle of catsup next to it. She frowned. Bill, who liked a neat house, usually picked up after himself.

"Hi Bill," she said softly.

"Hi," he said without turning his head.

She looked around the room. "Where's Allison?"

"She's at a friend's house."

"All right," Raymie said, making an effort not to be too testy. "Which friend?"

"God, Raymie, I don't know. Probably that girl down the street who lives with her dumpy grandmother."

Raymie blew out a breath. "So, how was your day at work?"

"Left early because I was feeling lousy."

"Oh, I'm sorry to hear that. How's your glucose level?"

"Way high."

"That's not good. Did you call the doctor?"

"No."

"Do you want me to?"

"I don't know. Who cares?" He took a long sip from his glass, gave a little grimace. "It's not getting any better so why bother."

Raymie sat down beside him and picked up the bottle to look more closely at the label. "This is a different brand than you usually get."

"Yeah," he said, eyes trained on the flashing screen before him.

Keeping her voice light, noncommittal, Raymie said, "Did you just buy it today?" When he didn't answer she set the bottle down with a sigh. "You know that alcohol is a really bad idea for someone with diabetes." She reached over to touch his arm, hoping to get him to turn to her. When he didn't, she said, "I don't know, Bill, I guess I just don't get it. Why do you keep drinking when it's so bad for you?"

He looked at her from inside eyes rimmed with red. "Well, Raymie, figure it out. Maybe I drink because it helps with this fucking pain."

Raymie was startled by the depth of agony in his eyes. She wondered if he'd been crying, but knew better than to ask. Slumping back, she took a breath and softened her voice. "Okay, I get that, I mean, I can tell that you've been in a lot of pain from the neuropathy. You can't get to sleep at night because your feet hurt so bad, right?"

He nodded. A small nod.

She leaned her head back against the nubby fabric of the

couch, weary. "Look, I think we should consult your doctor about this to see if maybe there's some kind of alternative. I don't want to nag or anything, but I'm getting worried about how much you're drinking."

"You worry too much, Raymie," he said, moving his shoulders to get more comfortable, to dismiss her, and returned his eyes to the television set.

Raymie sat looking at him, realizing that there was no hope of a reasonable discussion about it this evening. She let the subject go, swallowing the anger pushing at her throat. "Do you want me to cook tonight?" she said, reaching for an upbeat note.

"That would be fine." His voice was flat.

"I'll get started and then I'll go find Allison."

"Okay." Bill sipped his drink, then picked up the remote to switch the channel, turning the volume up at the same time.

That night, Raymie noticed that she was banging dishes while she washed them, and realized that she was definitely losing patience. Yes, Bill was sick. She felt really bad for him and was trying her best to make allowances. But whenever she reached for him, he pushed her away. This marriage, an unequal bargain to start with, was becoming a burden. And, really, it wouldn't be so bad for her if Bill would only let her in, let her offer him some comfort.

25

TWO YEARS LATER, Raymie sat in her living room under the bright light of the floor lamp, squinting at the shirt she was trying to mend. Her mind was on Allison, who had started community college in Seattle that fall. They had talked on the phone the night before, Allison's excitement over her new classes bringing freshness to Raymie's stale life.

She heard Bill limp into the room. He stood there, hesitant. "Raymie?"

She set down her sewing. "Bill? Are you okay?"

He was quiet a moment before he said. "I'll need a ride to that doctor appointment today."

Alarmed, Raymie turned off the lamp and stood up quickly. This was unusual. Raymie rarely drove anymore. Her vision was so poor that it was understood that Bill would do most of the driving. "Okay," she said, "let me get my coat. Can I get yours for you?"

Sitting side by side in the institutional metal-framed chairs of the waiting room, Bill surprised Raymie by reaching for her hand.

She looked over to see him hunched forward, staring blankly at the floor in front of him. After a while he spoke, his voice sounding husky, choked. "Raymie, I'm scared."

"Are you thinking about that guy you talked to?"

"Yeah, that diabetic who had to have his leg amputated. He said it started with a wound that wouldn't heal, just like what I have here."

"Oh, but it will be all right, Bill. It's got to be! The doctor will stop the infection, don't you think?"

"I sure as hell hope so."

"Well, of course you know that whatever happens, I'll be there, Bill."

He nodded and sucked in his breath. "Okay."

The music playing in the office came to Raymie's awareness, a song that she and Bill had both loved in the days they were first together. Bill looked at her and gave her a little smile, letting her know that he heard it too. It was from his favorite Jethro Tull album, one he knew by heart. He liked to sing along with the raunchier songs in an off-key half shout, but this little song was soft, elegant in its simplicity. His voice had always been gently teasing when he sang the lyrics to her:

Wondering aloud,
Would the years
treat us well?
As she floats in the kitchen,
I'm tasting the smell
of toast as the butter runs,
then she comes,
spilling crumbs,
on the bed.
And I shake my head.

He never sang the concluding lines, but Raymie knew he felt them even if he never could say them:

And it's only the giving
That makes you
What you are.

As they listened to the song together, Raymie remembered what she had lost sight of. Bill, in his own gruff way, loved her for who she was; he just never had the ability to express it.

Raymie put her head on Bill's shoulder, feeling the warmth through the fabric of his shirt, breathing in his familiar scent. He didn't reach over to stroke her hair as she longed for, but at the same time, he didn't shrug her off. And that was okay. The important thing was that he was willing, at least for today, to accept what she had to give.

26

Poulsbo, Washington, October 2013

"This is quite ridiculous," Raymie muttered to herself, wiping off the lipstick she'd just applied. She was reading way too much into this casual invitation, game night at Marcie and Jack's house. Nonetheless, she fluffed up her hair and put on her favorite earrings before turning to put away the clothing strewn across the bed—blouses she had considered, then decided were too dressy, too dowdy or too sexy.

When the doorbell rang, she grabbed her coat and went to answer it.

And there they were, Jack and Marcie, standing side by side at the door, coats buttoned up against the chill air. She opened the door wide to invite them in.

"Hi Rainy!" Marcie said. She stepped over the threshold to wrap her in a big hug.

"It's good to see you, Marcie," Raymie told her as they drew apart. "And you too, Jack." She momentarily caught his gaze before ducking her head to hide the heat rising to her cheeks.

"Good to see you too." Eyes moving past her into the interior, he said, "Great house."

"Oh, yes, thank you! I really love it, even though it's getting a bit scuffed up." She stepped back. "Please come on in. I just need to get my tote bag." Raymie led them into her kitchen. "I'm bringing a deck of oversized playing cards and a Sorry game with large game pieces," she chattered nervously. "I'm also bringing some fruit—strawberries—although the strawberries won't be as good this time of the year. Apples are really the best fall fruit. They have that extra snap to them that you don't get any other time of the year." Raymie looked at the strawberries packed in the tote. "Maybe I should have brought apples too."

Jack took the tote from her. "I know what you mean about the apples, but strawberries are a real treat this time of year."

Marcie said, "I love strawberries! And Jack and me made cheese and crackers."

"What, no Twinkies?" Raymie said in mock dismay.

"Hey! I like those! I like those little cupcakes that you get at the store too, but Lisa used to say they had a shelf-life of forever and that makes them bad for you." She rubbed at her nose with her sleeve. "Why is it that everything you really like is supposed to be bad for you? I don't get it."

"It doesn't seem particularly fair, does it?" Raymie commiserated, giving her friend a teasing grin.

Jack had put a leaf into the small kitchen table, making it large enough for the three of them to play cards comfortably, but crowding the kitchen a bit. As Raymie entered the room, Sheba wandered in, her pretty little face turned up toward them to mew for attention and treats. Raymie bent down to stroke her silky fur and she leaned, serpentine, into Raymie's hand.

The dogs were also in attendance, although Jack had assigned the large, shaggy Shep to a particular corner so he wouldn't be too underfoot. Shep circled the spot a couple of times, then curled up, looking satisfied.

"Shep seems like such a good dog," Raymie noted as she

settled into a chair.

"Yeah, he really is," Jack said. Marcie handed him the plate of cheese and crackers. As he leaned forward to place it on the table, Raymie saw the pattern of his shirt, a nice flannel plaid, so comfortable.

"He's our sixth dog," Marcie said.

"We always had dogs when the boys were growing up," Jack told her as he set the bowl of strawberries next to the cheese plate. "And then there was this gap of a few years before we got Shep."

"Yeah, we had Sunny before that, and after the boys moved away, she was mostly Lisa's dog," Marcie said, taking her place at the table. "She loved us all, but Lisa was her special favorite."

"Sunny died several months before Lisa," Jack said slowly. "I thought that Lisa was going to have a really hard time with that, and she did, but she also said that it was okay with her because Sunny was paving the way, you know, showing her that it was all right to let go." He sat down, a sad smile crossing his face. "I guess that's when I finally let myself know that we were going to lose Lisa." He caught Raymie's sympathetic gaze. "Sorry," he said. "I don't know why I'm telling you this. Not a happy subject for conversation."

"Oh, no, I don't mind at all, I'm actually kind of glad that you feel comfortable telling me about it."

"Marcie told me that you lost your husband a few years back."

Raymie nodded and he gave her a rueful smile of understanding.

Marcie said, "It was hard to think about getting another dog after Sunny. We were so sad we couldn't even think about a new pet."

"Oh, I know what you mean," Raymie told her. "We love our

pets so much and they leave us all too soon. There's a poem I like about that that, which goes, 'Brothers and sisters, I bid you beware, of giving your heart to a dog to tear.'"

"Ah!" Jack said, brightening up, "Rudyard Kipling. That's my favorite poem of his. I sometimes use it in class."

"Oh, mine too!"

"So, do you read a lot of poetry?" he asked.

"Well, not as much as I used to. When I was in college, I used to read quite a bit, and I mostly chose to read poetry in my oral interpretation class. I love the rhythm of a poem; it's like music to me, and I like the way the spoken images sort of burn themselves in your mind, if that makes any sense."

"Yes, absolutely," Jack said, with obvious interest. "I think that you put it very well."

"Jack writes poems," Marcie said, popping a strawberry into her mouth.

"Oh, I did when I was younger. These days I mostly just teach poetry classes."

"I'd love to read some of your poems!" Raymie told him, eager to read something of his. "I mean, if you want to share them."

"I guess I could dig something up," he said evasively. "They're somewhere in my room. You know, up in the apartment over the garage. It would take me awhile to find them."

Raymie hadn't meant to put him on the spot. "Oh, yes, that's fine. Maybe another time."

He seemed grateful for that suggestion. "Sure, no problem. I'll see what I can find." The tension Raymie had heard in his voice relaxed. He held up the cards. "What would you two like to play?"

"Crazy eights!" Marcie exclaimed, gently setting Sheba, who

she had taken into her lap on the floor.

Jack looked at Raymie for confirmation and she said, "I'd love to, but I'll need some reminders about the rules."

"I'll help you," Marcie said.

They were settled at the kitchen table playing their third game of crazy eights when the dogs stood at attention, noses pointed toward the door. There was a short knock, then the creak of the door opening.

"Halloo! It's me, Cindy!"

Jack looked startled and Marcie said something under her breath that Raymie didn't quite catch. They heard the clip of high heels, then a woman wearing a long pale coat, worn open to reveal a good figure in a fitted dress, walked into the room, a plate held aloft like a prize. "I was on my way to a party and I thought I'd stop by with some cookies for Marcie and her friend."

She looked at Raymie. "I'm Cindy," she said, the volume of her voice going up a notch.

"Nice to meet you." Standing, Raymie offered her hand. Cindy responded with a tiny imitation of a handshake, offering only her fingertips.

Cindy placed the cookies on the counter. "Are you enjoying your game?" She waved her hand toward the cookies. "These are snicker doodles. I hope you like them. Marcie does, don't you?"

When Marcie didn't answer Raymie said, "They look very yummy. Thank you."

"Well," Cindy said breezily, "I've got to run. Just thought I'd stop by."

Jack, who had stood up at the same time as Raymie, told Cindy, "I'll walk you to your car."

27

AS SOON AS THEY walked out the door, Cindy leaned her head conspiratorially toward Jack. "Marcie's friend seems almost normal, doesn't she? I mean you'd hardly know she's got that defect except for the dog and the big playing cards."

"Oh, for Christ's sake, Cindy," Jack said in annoyance. "What's normal? She seems normal enough to me, and so does Marcie, for that matter. They're both pretty nice people. Isn't that what's important?"

"Now babe, don't be testy," she coaxed, brushing something off his shoulder.

She pursed her lips. "You know, this shirt is getting pretty worn out, maybe we'd better replace it. Besides, plaid flannel is so, I don't know, lumberjack."

Jack sighed, turned his head.

She stepped back. "What is it, Jack? You're different with me lately. I mean, I've been trying to ignore it but there sure seems to be some kind of disconnect going on." She saw Jack hesitate, searching for a reply. "What?" she said, "Isn't this good for you anymore?"

Her perfume, as always, was too strong. "I don't know. This isn't a good time to talk about it."

Cindy narrowed her eyes, "What exactly do you mean? What's going on? You just haven't been there for me lately." She drew in a breath. "I mean, like tonight. You knew how important this party was to me, I told you about it at least a week ago, but you chose to do game night. Game night. Really?"

Jack was looking up the street.

"Jack?"

He turned his head to look at her. "I told you then that we'd already made plans."

"We? Who is we? Marcie and her little blind friend? Quite honestly, Jack, you have a way of siding with these . . . no, I'm not going to say it because I'm afraid of what I might say."

He turned more completely to face her. "Go ahead and say it. You've wanted to for a while."

She sighed in exasperation. "Listen, the people at this party tonight, they're important career contacts for me and I really wanted you there. But you felt obligated to hang out with Marcie and her pal."

"I'm sorry, Cindy, but I don't have very much in common with those people." He shrugged. "But look, you're going to be fine without me tonight. Go mingle. Chances are you'll meet some guy who just wows you with his designer clothes and big career plans." He watched her face harden and tried to soften what he was saying to her. "Let's face it, you're dissatisfied with me. You keep pushing me to do more, to get more recognition for my work, more money, more status. Sometimes it seems like that's all you care about."

Cindy crossed her arms, "Really, Jack, don't you think you're exaggerating just a little bit?"

"No, I don't. I keep trying to tell you this and you don't want to hear it." He slowed his voice for emphasis. "Like I keep telling you, I'm looking forward to retiring in a few more years and just enjoying life. You know, sitting down with a cup of coffee and a good book. Stepping out on the porch to feel the air on my face and to watch the sun rise."

And suddenly this idyllic scene from Jack's future, which he'd tried and failed to fit Cindy into, had another person in it, standing beside him on the back porch. He saw his arm go around her, saw himself kiss the top of her strawberry-blond head, silver strands twined among the soft curls. Raymie, he thought with a shock of joy. Oh, my God. Of course. Raymie!

He looked at Cindy, finding it hard to focus on her face, knowing this wasn't fair to her.

Cindy's voice became quiet. "So that's how it is, huh? You want me to go hook up with somebody more ambitious and you're going to have this nice retirement sitting on your butt with your nose in a book. Is that right, Jack?"

He wasn't sure what to say. This was happening so fast. Suddenly he was aware of the unraveling that had been going on between them for some time now. And with that realization was this new feeling pulling at him, the resonance he felt with Raymie. He stood there, a sense of unreality making his body feel light.

Cindy got into her car, slamming the door behind her.

28

Raymie heard the door open softly. Jack walked into the kitchen, looking stunned.

Marcie quipped, "Hey, what's wrong? You two break up or something?"

"Let's finish the game," he said.

Marcie looked up at him from where she was sitting at the table, surprise altering her voice. "You did, didn't you?"

He shrugged. "We can talk about that later, Marcie. Right now we have a guest." He took his seat at the table, eyes averted, and picked up his cards.

"We don't have to finish the game," Raymie offered.

"No, please, let's finish the game. He looked up at her from over his cards, his eyes dark. "I'm sorry, that couldn't have been very comfortable for you."

"Oh, no, I'm okay. Just, perhaps you'd like some time to yourself right now?"

"I'd rather play. Whose turn is it?"

It was Jack's turn. Marcie got up and walked to the counter. She picked up a cookie, took a bite. "Well, I will miss her cookies."

Jack looked up, annoyed. "I thought you didn't like Cindy."

"Well, but she does make good cookies."

The ride back to Raymie's house was mostly quiet, with small spurts of careful conversation. Raymie had offered the front seat to Marcie, who said no, she preferred to sit in the back with Shainy. Raymie was glad of that. She wanted to sit next to Jack, to imagine the warmth of his body on the other side of the seat, to see the outline of his profile in the passing headlights and to hear the soft slide of his hands as he shifted them on the steering wheel.

When Jack pulled up in front of the house Raymie opened the door on her side, getting out before Jack could decide whether or not he should open it for her.

Jack got out and retrieved Raymie's tote from where he'd stashed it in the trunk. "It's a pretty dark night," he observed, looking at the sky. "Would you like me to walk you to your door?"

Raymie smiled, tempted, but her independent streak got the better of her. "I think that Shainy and I have the walk to the front door down," she said, taking the tote from his hand.

Nodding, Jack opened the rear door to let Shainy out. Marcie got out on her side to give Raymie a big hug.

When she released her, Raymie said, "Thanks for the nice time, you two. See you on the bus, Marcie."

"The next game night is in two weeks," Marcie blurted out. "We want you to come."

"Two weeks?" Jack asked Marcie.

"No, not two weeks, a week!" Marcie said, "Let's do it again next week!"

She looked at Jack, then at Raymie. "Usually we do game night one time a month, but I don't want to wait that long."

Jack said, "What do you think, Raymie? Are you free next Friday?" His voice was coaxing, playful, as he added, "We could make you dinner."

"Well, yes, I'd love to do game night again next week," she said, the joy flashing through her. "And dinner sounds wonderful." She hesitated, then added, "Oh, and please call me Rainy if you like. I kind of like my new nickname."

"Well, see you next Friday then, Rainy."

The sound of his voice saying the name felt like a caress. "Me and my big cards?"

Jack laughed.

It took everything Raymie had to resist the urge to reach out and touch his hand, to curl her fingers around his.

29

THAT NIGHT JACK couldn't sleep. He shifted in his bed, pulling the covers closer, acutely aware of their texture, the hush of their movement over the mattress, the wind outside moving the trees, the dance of light behind his eyes, not quite a dream. He felt vibrantly alive, his body crackling with the electricity of sensation.

A poem was pushing at the edge of his mind, and he found himself arranging and rearranging the words, twisting their position, searching for alternatives, just the right phrase.

After an hour or two he threw the blankets aside and put on the clothes he had draped over the chair next to his bed. He went to the sink to get a glass of water, then to the desk on the other side of the studio apartment above the garage that served as his bedroom. He sat at his computer and started to write.

Hours later, the first light of day was graying the sky as he walked over to the house to make his morning coffee.

Steaming cup in hand, he stepped out to the covered deck overlooking the backyard. It had started to rain softly and as the sun rose, Jack saw raindrops making tiny circles as they met the water of the little creek partway down the yard.

Watching the gentle dance of raindrops on the water, he remembered how much Lisa had loved that creek, the memory bringing with it the image of his sons' small feet as they waded in its quiet flow.

So long ago.

Marcie came up beside him looking disheveled, the belt of her blue rope tucked tightly at her round middle.

"Hey there, Marcie," he said.

"Hi Jack." She yawned, giving her arms a stretch. "How did you sleep?"

"I don't think I slept at all."

"I was wondering about that. I saw the apartment lights on when I got up to pee." She paused. "You were thinking about Rainy, weren't you?"

Jack looked at her, startled. "How did you know?"

"Oh, that's easy. I saw how you two looked at each other. She likes you too, you know."

Jack exhaled shakily.

"Are you scared?" Marcie asked, touching his arm.

"Oh, well, only slightly terrified," he said with a nervous laugh.

"Are you afraid she'll die too? Like Lisa?"

"Oh, yes, that and a lot of other things."

"It's going to be okay, Jack," Marcie said, gazing out at the rain.

He turned to her, amused. "I don't understand it, Marcie—you seem so wise sometimes. Aren't you supposed to be a little slow?"

Marcie's laugh was more of a snort. "You don't have to be smart to know what things go together. We belong together, me, you and Rainy."

They stood together, watching the rain. Jack sipping his coffee.

After a while, Marcie said, "Look at it this way, Jack. Maybe this time you'll be the first one to die."

Jack choked on his coffee, laughter pushing up from deep in his gut. "That's a comforting thought," he joked, and then realized that what he had just said was actually true.

Jack hadn't known that he'd been holding himself so rigid until he felt his muscles loosen. Yawning, he decided he would make Marcie and himself a big, greasy breakfast, then it was back to bed for him. He knew that he would be able to sleep after that.

Flipping eggs while Marcie buttered the toast, Jack thought about how hard it had been to lose Lisa. He figured he must have gone into some kind of full-on clinical depression after her death. Nothing had interested him, nothing tasted good, he just wanted to lay in bed all day and sleep.

Marcie's question interrupted his thoughts: "Want jam, Jack?"

"No thanks." He paused. "Actually, no, I'll have some. Slather it on! Let's have jam!"

She laughed and his thoughts returned to the months after Lisa's death. Thank God for Marcie, who forced his butt out of bed and made him shower and shave and go to work. She and the boys, who were pretty busy with their own lives, did whatever they could to pull him out of it, and eventually it worked. But there was this gray fog that hung over his life since then, and he sometimes felt like he was sleepwalking, moving through his day woodenly. Until now. Last night it felt like he had finally woken up and once again saw the world with all of his senses alive and alert.

He slid the eggs onto a plate, his mind returning to the past, reviewing his life with Lisa. He'd known her for so long, since his college days at the U. She had been his greatest love. Oh sure, there were girls before her, casual high-school girlfriends, and that woman from his art class, but in the end, it was Lisa who had taken his heart.

The thing was, his life with Lisa hadn't been all that great. There were plenty of good times, but there was also a lot of pain. His eyes softened and a smile played at the corners of his mouth. Lisa was truly a force to be reckoned with. It had been a wild ride that didn't seem to slow down until the later years.

And then, she was gone.

"Here are your eggs, Marcie," he said, handing her the plate.

"Thanks, Jack! And here's your toast."

Jack looked at the toast. Marcie had indeed slathered on the jam. It was heaped on top of the toast to the point that it was dripping off the sides.

"Very funny, Marcie," he said, gingerly taking the toast between his thumb and forefinger.

She looked at him with mock innocence, then broke into a sheepish grin.

30

Seattle, Washington, 1973

Jack would always associate the University of Washington with the last fine days of autumn. Days when the intake of a breath would feel a little cleaner with the cooled air. When the slanted light made bright streaks across grass dotted with the first yellow leaves of the season, the sound of purposeful footsteps moving briskly in myriad directions across the red brick of the campus walkways, the murmur of low voices like a river with the occasional high note of a called-out greeting rising above the flow.

The artfully grouped bouquet of cherry trees in bloom on either side of the quad were strikingly beautiful in the spring, but it was always those sunny fall days that would come back to him in his memories, with their sense of both a new beginning and a return to old, known patterns, the long held academic traditions, as books were picked up again and clean notebooks readied for the first penned lines.

The Suzzallo library, a prominent feature of the large red brick-covered square affectionately known as "Red Square" that marked the main campus entry was Jack's favorite place to study. The reading room with its long, lamp-lit tables and high arched ceiling was impressive in its vastness and beauty, but Jack liked best to find a comfortable little table among the stacks, where he would take occasional breaks from disciplined study to leaf through the yellowed pages of old volumes, their musty smell a welcome aroma that spoke of ideas and images long past.

Despite his professors' enthusiastic praise for the essays he wrote, papers that fairly sang with the passion he felt for literature, Jack was perplexed to find himself something of a star in his English classes. So many of the other students came from wealthier homes than his and many had learned about classic literature at an early age; surely, they would have the advantage, he thought. Yet having never heard of Camus or Tolstoy before they were introduced to him at college, Jack was able to see these works through fresh and inspired eyes and turned in papers that glowed with insights that were missed by those who were used to seeing them on their parents' bookshelves.

His success in his English classes gained Jack some notoriety among his peers, and he formed friendships with those who were also enamored with the written word and the creation of story. His friend Damien, who was really named Dennis but took the name Damien from the Herman Hesse novel, invited Jack to take one of the vacant rooms in the large ramshackle house that Damien shared with four other students. The house reminded Jack of the one he lived in as a child, and Jack, feeling right at home in a room with the bed tucked under the slanted ceiling, moved in at Christmas break. His housemates were an easygoing mix and Jack easily fell into the rhythm of the household, eating his meals at a wobbly old table in the shared dining room, sometimes communally and sometimes by himself with a book propped up in front of his plate.

It was in the cavernous classroom where his geology class

met that Jack's attention was first drawn to an attractive dark-haired woman who often chose a seat near his.

Observing her in brief glances, trying not to stare too openly, he was impressed by her vitality, the way she bustled around, arranging her books on her desk, turning to check in with other students with quick wry quips about the class, her eyes straying briefly to Jack, to see if he was watching, he thought. He found her quite beautiful, with dusky olive skin, high cheekbones and thick curly hair threatening to burst from its tie-back. "Earth Mother" had become a popular term to describe round, curvaceous women and she definitely fit that description, with wide hips and bottom, narrow waist and large breasts. Her arms and legs were a bit on the stubby side and didn't quite fit her torso, giving her a foreshortened look that stole from this picture of perfection. Still, the overall effect was of a charming sturdiness, a Shetland pony rather than an appaloosa, and beautiful in her own right. A girl who always drew stares, she played on her good qualities, affecting not to notice or care about the attention paid to her good looks.

When in the third week their Geology class broke up into small groups, Jack took note of which direction she was moving and went to join the same group. She had already claimed a seat and when he caught her glance, she turned her eyes to the chair next to hers. Jack sat down.

"So okay," the girl said when they all were seated, immediately taking a leadership role, "we should all introduce ourselves. I'm Lisa."

As soon as everyone had murmured a name Lisa jumped in again to say, "I think that the effect of human intervention on the geological process is a hugely relevant topic for discussion." She drew a breath and looked around the circle of faces to make sure she had everyone's attention. "There is no end to the harm that we have done to our environment and it has certainly screwed with the natural geological process." She leaned forward in her chair, drawing the others toward her as she said, "To start with, I think strip mining is a big factor. Any other ideas?"

"Dredging could be a contributor," the girl next to her said, and several students nodded in agreement.

"Good. Any other thoughts?" Lisa asked.

One of the students in the group was sitting back in his chair, arms crossed over his chest. "I think that it's easy to point a finger at the mining industry but we need to weigh the benefits we receive from that industry against the minor harm it does to the environment."

Lisa turned to him, her eyes flashing, the perfect embodiment of Artemis, her bow poised for the kill. "Oh really? And should we condone the methods they use that create this minor harm?" Lisa said, her voice raising in volume and intensity. "Of course, creating a wasteland where there once was forest would be a minor problem to people who think profit is more important than conserving our natural resources."

"Well, I wasn't quite saying that."

"What exactly were you saying then?" Lisa said, staring hard at him.

Everyone became still, watching for the outcome of this face-off, their group a pool of frozen silence in the midst of the noisy classroom.

Jack hadn't noticed that he was holding his breath until the professor leaned into the group to ask how it was going and to remind them to choose someone to take notes.

As the professor stepped away Jack broke the silence by

suggesting that dikes and dams could have an effect. Lisa looked at him with a little annoyance, but her adversary looked relieved, and the discussion continued without further conflict.

Happy now just to observe, Jack offered to take notes, knowing that in that role it would be easy to watch Lisa, who continued to take control of the discussion.

He liked the way she dressed. She was wearing a brightly colored peasant blouse, braless as was the custom in those bra-burning days, and bell-bottomed jeans that were a bit too long, with embroidered hems that crumpled over her red Converse shoes. She had topped this ensemble off with a man's navy pea-coat, also a little too long. Jack found the effect enchanting. The tomboyish exterior belied the round figure beneath her clothes, the feminine curve of her neck, the turn of her wrists, her small soft hands half-hidden by the cuffs of the large coat.

Immersed in admiration, the disappointing sound of the professor announcing the end of the period broke through Jack's thoughts. He gathered up his books and the notes he'd taken and reluctantly moved toward the door, hoping to catch Lisa as she left the room.

Lisa came up beside him. "I'm meeting some friends at the Underground Exit," she told him. "Want to come along?"

"Sure. That would be great," he said, then hesitated before adding, "It's just that I can't stay long, I have to work this afternoon."

"Where're you working?"

"The drug store at U Ave and 45th."

"Oh yeah, I know the place," she said. "Kind of a bourgeois establishment, isn't it?"

Jack shrugged. "It's a job."

She nodded. "Well, come for as long as you can."

"What about you? Do you have a job?" Jack asked as they started to move down the hall.

"Me? No. I do some volunteering. Mostly I just concentrate on school. My folks foot the bill, which is cool, but I get tired of them trying to run the show. You know what I mean?"

"Sure," was Jack's noncommittal response. A rich girl, he thought with a twinge of disappointment. He hoped that didn't make her out of his league.

Lisa led the way to a coffee shop just off campus. "Here we are," she said.

She yanked open the heavy door and something in the angle of her body as she tugged, the flush of determination on her face, pulled at Jack and he felt tenderness, protectiveness and admiration stir within him. He caught the edge of the door to hold it for her as she entered.

The coffee shop wasn't exactly subterranean, but it felt that way, located as it was in the vast daylight basement of this ancient building just off the campus grounds. There were small rectangular windows placed high in the wall on one side of the room, cloudy with residue from cigarette smoke and neglect. The long tables down the center of the room were of unvarnished wood, flanked by chairs of every description from slouchy comfortable to straight-backed severe. These tables, as well as the smaller tables along the periphery, were stained with coffee and gouged with graffiti. They were laden with coffee in heavy earthenware mugs, plates of edibles, overflowing ashtrays, books, newspapers, arms and elbows. The thick rough-wood posts that unabashedly held up the low plaster ceiling were covered in posters and notices, some curling off, others newly thumbtacked to the surface.

Standing at the doorway, Jack was washed with a wave of voices, some soft, some deep and resonant, some urgently loud, interspersed with the clink of dishes and the hiss of coffee preparation. And beneath it all was the buried sound of music, maybe jazz, Jack thought, or perhaps rock and roll or maybe even folk—it was hard to tell.

He inhaled deeply to take in the smell of dark-roasted coffee and the roof of his mouth tingled in anticipation of that first sip as Lisa looked around for her friends.

"Oh there they are!" she said, pointing toward a full table where an arm was waving above the heads. She took Jack by the sleeve and pulled him along with her, dodging around the crowded tables with practiced ease. A few people moved aside to make room at the already full table and they took seats directly across from one another, which pleased Jack because he could look into her face and catch the interest in her eyes. She settled in, saying hello to the people she knew and asking the names of those she didn't. Then she moved her eyes around the faces at the table and said, "Hey, everybody, meet Jack. Jack, this is everybody." There were several hearty greetings and a few people told him their names, most of which Jack promptly forgot in his distracted desire to catch Lisa's eye. When she moved her gaze to his he smiled at her and she smiled back, her look of surprised wonder at the pleasure it gave her mirroring his own.

The conversation at the table turned quickly to politics. Earlier in the month congress had formed the Select Committee on Presidential Campaign Activities to investigate President Nixon's involvement in the Watergate break-in. "Now the asshole is looking for an excuse to disband the committee," one of the guys at the table said in disgust.

"That's because," one of the other guys said in a decent imitation of Nixon's already famous speech, "I am not a crook."

There was a smattering of laughter and a few groans in appreciation of the impression, and in the pause that followed, Lisa leaned forward, scanning the faces of everyone at the crowded table. "Okay," she said, "But let's set Nixon aside for now. I think the Lakota Sioux protest at Wounded Knee is currently of more importance."

The table quieted. The man next to her asked, "Is anybody here going to Wounded Knee to support them?"

"I was thinking about going at spring break," one of the guys said.

"That might be too late," the girl sitting next to Jack said.

"I'm planning to go in a little less than two weeks. My friend Morse is taking his car and we have a couple of extra seats for anyone who wants to come along." Heads turned toward a man with a large Afro sitting at the end of the table. Jack noticed Lisa smile possessively at the guy and felt a spark of jealousy, but also admiration. Did Lisa date this guy? That was brave, with so many bigots out there. He hoped that they hadn't been harassed when they were out together. Then he thought, "But if she's with him why does she seem so interested in me?"

He heard Lisa say, "Then I guess I'm going to go with you. It won't kill me to miss some school. This is more important."

Jack noticed with irritation that his jealous feelings had deepened. He pushed at an empty plate to hide his annoyance.

The girl on his right turned to him. "So, do you support the cause of the Lakota people?" she asked quietly.

He hesitated. "Actually I don't know a whole lot about it, but what little I do know makes it sound like a legitimate cause."

The girl raised an eyebrow and tipped her head in

question. "You haven't been listening to the news? This is a big deal. They're occupying Wounded Knee to protest about the conditions at the reservation, and now our government is treating them like criminals."

"Well you see, I'm an English major," he said in explanation. "I'm pretty well immersed in all the reading and writing I've been assigned."

"So, does that mean you can't take the time to be politically informed?" The girl asked, her eyes hard. She had caught the attention of a couple of other people at the table who were looking at Jack with interest.

"Well, yes, I guess that's no excuse," Jack said, uncomfortable. "But if you want to know more about Virginia Woolf's use of stream of consciousness, I could tell you a whole lot about that."

Lisa, who had been watching the interchange, came to his defense. "Most of us here are Poli-Sci majors, Susan, so of course we know about the Wounded Knee situation in detail. Jack seems to know as much as the average person. It's our responsibility to educate people about what's happening, not to criticize them."

"She's right, Susan," one of the guys at the table said. Then he narrowed his eyes at Jack, looking puzzled before his face lit up in recognition. "Oh, I remember you!" he said. "You're that hot-shot in my Shakespeare class that the prof is so impressed with."

"I don't know if he's all that impressed," Jack muttered, something between pleased and embarrassed.

"So, anyway," the girl said, turning to the rest of the people grouped around the table, "what can those of us who aren't able to go to Wounded Knee do here? Is anyone circulating pamphlets or raising money?"

Different ideas were proffered and discussed with Lisa a main contributor to the discussion. Jack listened with pleasure as Lisa spoke with intelligence and enthusiasm, content just to be near her. After an hour passed, Jack drank the last of his coffee and reluctantly said, "I've got to get to work." He looked at the other people at the table. "It was good to meet you," then turned to Lisa to say, "Thanks for inviting me." He hesitated, trying to figure out a way to casually ask to get together with her again, when the girl who had been sitting on Jack's right drew Lisa's attention away with a question about the trip to South Dakota to join the Wounded Knee occupation.

Jack had swung his backpack on a shoulder and had turned to go when he felt Lisa grab his wrist. "Let's do this again," she said, "Tuesday after class?"

31

RIGHT FROM THE START it was primarily Lisa's friends they hung out with, sitting in noisy, crowded bars or coffee shops, where political opinions were expressed in loud, excited voices. Jack shared enough of their views to fit in and take part in their discussions, even participating in a few marches. But really, what he wanted most was just to be with Lisa, to sit elbow to elbow with her and listen to her talk, riding the waves of her emotional highs and lows as she pushed forward ideas on topics that were so vitally important to her.

On occasion Jack and Lisa spent a relatively quiet evening with one or two of Jack's friends, friends that shared his interests in literature, art and music, quiet individuals who were respectful of his occasional need for solitude, understanding that time for reflection was vital to him because they shared the same need. His friends liked Lisa: "You are one lucky dog to have found brains and beauty in the same package!" they told Jack, but he could tell that her energy was a bit much for them sometimes. She was loud and opinionated and always said exactly what she thought, not caring who she might offend. At the end of an evening he could sense that his friends were relieved that he and Lisa were leaving so they could fold back into themselves and return to the quiet solace that Lisa's forceful nature intruded upon.

For her part, Lisa liked Jack's friends but found them a little nerdy and dull. She didn't entirely understand the need for solitude, but she accepted that Jack required a certain amount of time to himself, and for Jack that acceptance was enough; she didn't have to understand. Lisa had plenty of friends, so that when Jack needed to withdraw, she simply picked up the phone and found someone who wanted to talk. She learned that he had no problem with the full calendar she kept as long as she was with him by the end of the day.

Just as Lisa said what she pleased, she also dressed as she pleased, choosing her wardrobe, like her words, for effect. One morning during the first months of their relationship, the subject of clothing came up while she was getting ready for class. Probing for the pierced hole where she was attempting to shove the end of the huge earring that would complete her usual eclectic attire, this time a red peasant blouse topped by a bright multicolored tunic, she told him that her mother, who he hadn't met yet, was always after her about her appearance. "From the time I was allowed to choose my own clothes she hated how I dressed." Lisa picked up her other earring. "When I was little, she'd buy me these silly ruffled dresses, with shiny Mary Janes to go with them." She put a finger to her cheek and batted her eyes to mimic a prissy little girl, then her expression turned to disgust. "After a while, I refused to even try them on. I could tell that Mom was disappointed, but no matter how hard she tried she wasn't going to mold me into some proper little lady." Lisa looked at Jack's reflection in the mirror. He nodded to let her know he was paying attention. "My dad is mostly Irish, but my mom was born in Greece, did I tell you that? My grandparents came to America when she was just a baby." Lisa frowned. "I don't know, but maybe because she was the daughter of immigrants, Mom developed this overriding need to fit in." Lisa shrugged. "Anyway, Mom was always telling us kids that we should strive to go a step further than the average person." Lisa picked up a brush that was sitting on the bathroom sink, his roommate's actually, but Jack decided to let it go, and yanked it vigorously through her thick hair. "You know, better dressed, better educated, more financially successful." Lisa set the brush down and turned away from the sink. "But that's not me, not me at all. I have no interest in the whole competition thing, having to always be the best. That's her game, not mine."

Lisa strode out of the bathroom, Jack moving aside to let her through, and grabbed her books off the dining room table. "Well, that's enough of that. We need to get to class," she said. "Better get your stuff."

Jack took his gray sweater off the hook by the door and pulled it over his t-shirt, feeling drab next to Lisa in her colorful outfit. He watched the brightly striped over-sized tunic swing around Lisa's hips as she walked—no, marched—ahead of him. Jack smiled to himself, thinking that going a step further than the average person was exactly what Lisa did, but not in the way her mother intended. For Lisa, that meant being more radical, more outspoken, smarter, tougher.

Beneath the tough exterior was an unrepentant flirt. Lisa never passed up an opportunity to *ooh* over a puppy or baby or flirt with a small child, smiling sweetly and laying on the charm until the child shyly squirmed with joy. Jack enjoyed seeing these exchanges, but he didn't like it when she turned the same kind of attention toward other men. When he brought it up, she laughed at him saying, "I'm just playing around, you goose. Don't take it so seriously."

Jack tried not to let it get to him, but when she put her arm around some guy's neck to whisper in his ear it galled him, the jealousy that he tried to deny sweeping his face with the heat of frustrated anger. He knew that she didn't believe in monogamy in theory, but that didn't mean she would put that into practice, did it? Jack reminded himself that Lisa was just a very friendly person. He could tell that she adored him, partly because she so often told him that, and partly because of the way she looked at him, her eyes suddenly drawn to him in the middle of the chaos of conversation in a crowded room, pausing for a moment to smile at him in a way she smiled for no one else.

On a Sunday near the end of his senior year, Jack lay facedown on the couch, listening to the phone ring for the sixth time that day. He knew he should have been sitting at his typewriter, but he couldn't move, much less think about the paper he needed to write.

The phone was ringing for the seventh time when his roommate Damien, who had just returned home, picked up. "Oh, hi Lisa," Jack heard him say, "Yeah, he's here."

Jack shook his head vigorously.

"But I guess he's not able to talk right now." Damien was silent a moment, listening, "Okay, I'll pass that on. Take it easy, Lisa. See you tomorrow in class."

Damien set the receiver down. "Okay, what's going on Jack? Lisa said she's been trying to reach you all day." He looked closely at Jack. "Jesus, man, you look like shit. You two have a fight?"

"Something like that." Jack muttered, turning toward the backrest. His arms clenched around his middle, he cradled himself against the memory of Lisa leaving him behind, and within that memory was another one—the memory of himself as a six-year-old boy, a boy whose mother had left him. He saw himself standing with the front door open, looking out at the rain, hoping to see her hurrying down the walk, huddled against the downpour, rushing to take him in her arms. And his aunt's voice behind him. "You may as well close the door, Jack. She's not coming back."

The next day Lisa chased him as he strode through the campus square. She had called after him a couple of times and he'd ignored her, moving fast, eyes straight ahead.

She caught up with him, panting slightly from the effort. "Jack, what the hell is up with you?" Then slowing down, she said, "No, don't tell me. It's about Saturday night, isn't it?" She threw her hands up. "Oh please. Give me a break!"

Jack sucked in his cheeks, holding back the sob that was pushing at his throat. "Great deduction, Sherlock. How ever did you figure that out?"

"Slow down, Jack," she said, irritation in her voice. "You know I can't walk that fast."

He slowed down a little but still wouldn't look at her.

She walked beside him, frowning. "Well, shit," she said, shaking her head. "Listen Jack, I told you that I wasn't into this whole monogamy thing, okay? You seem to have this patriarchal belief that you have the right to own me and my body."

"It's not like that and you know it," he snapped.

"Oh yeah? What's it like then?"

He felt a tear escape and chose anger to suppress the rising grief. "It's about loving you, stupid." He stopped, turned toward her. "You're always hanging out with other guys, clutching their arms, laughing with them, and having these deep, very important conversations. And that's okay, I'm okay with that, but it would be natural, no, normal, for me not to want you to sleep with them." He took a deep breath to quell the fierce, raw love that was rising up, pushing at him. "Dammit, Lisa! I didn't invent this you know. People have practiced monogamy for centuries. Eons!"

"Oh yeah," she said, "sure. So that a man could be certain that his property and her children were exclusively his."

Jack shook his head. "Okay, so maybe that's part of it. But not for me. For me it's about loving someone so much that you just don't want them to share the same . . . I don't know, intensity, closeness, whatever you want to call what we have, Lisa, with someone else."

Lisa stood her ground, her face formed into a scowl. "The world is changing, Jack. Haven't you noticed that? The old ideas about marriage and child rearing are in the past. My life, my lifestyle choices—they are an embodiment of that change."

"Well," Jack said, "you're welcome to it." He turned to continue on his path to the building in front of him, then turned back, anger now flowing through him. "You know, Lisa, there are a lot of things you believe in that I agree with. But not this. Not this. I draw the line here."

He strode forward and she continued to follow him. "Go away, Lisa."

"But Jack, listen to reason."

"No!" he shouted. He sped up, moving quickly to the front doors. When he no longer felt her behind him, he veered to the back of the building. Alone, leaning against the rough brick wall, his books tossed to the grass, hands on knees, he was finally able to unleash the wracking sobs.

It took almost two weeks. When she approached him again

it wasn't an apology so much as a concession. She never openly took another lover, but Jack wasn't altogether sure she had stopped. He tried not to watch her too closely around other men, but the question was always there, following him around, making him feel diminished, anxious and on guard.

32

Seattle, Washington, 1975

The evening was brisk but lovely, the fading light glowing orange as it touched the tops of the Cascade mountains, the snow on Mount Rainier taking on the color of the sky. The days were slowly getting longer, each bringing them a little closer to spring. Jack took a deep breath of the cool air. It was the perfect time of the day for a quick walk to the corner grocery and he listened with pleasure to the sound of his footsteps on the dusky pavement, his arm swinging the paper bag he was carrying.

Opening the door to their apartment, he was immediately assaulted by the smell of cooking. "I'm in here!" Lisa called from the kitchen. The grocery bag made a nice crinkly sound as he set it on the worn oak table that they'd rescued from a neighbor who was going to haul it to the dump.

Jack smiled in satisfaction as he looked around him. He and Lisa had moved in together after graduation, both finding work as teachers—Jack at a public school teaching English, Lisa scraping by on her meager salary from an alternative private school. They found this small shabby apartment on Queen Anne hill that they both loved, with a view of the city and Elliott Bay. It was a lucky find; considering the gentrification going on all around them, a place with this kind of view probably wouldn't be available on a young college graduate's income in a few years' time. It was sparsely furnished but attractive in its own way. They had painted the walls, scrubbed the stained hardwood floor, put up art-print posters, making this small space their own.

Lisa, wearing a striped kaftan over a pair of worn jeans, was standing at the old bulbous stove that used up most of the space in their cramped kitchen. Busy with her cooking, she offered her cheek to kiss. Jack said, "I got the green pepper you wanted, but it's not in the best shape. The guy at the store said they'll have better ones tomorrow, but that doesn't help with tonight. How's it going, chef?"

"I'm not sure. The smell isn't giving me a lot of confidence." Lisa took a quizzical sip from the spoon she'd been using to stir the brownish mass in the pot before her. "Oh God, Jack! This is awful! It tastes worse than that thing you made last week—what was it called?"

"Hungarian Goulash."

"Well, whatever you did to that Hungarian, it might come under the heading of torture. That was really gross." She took another sip off the spoon she was holding, then making a face, threw the spoon petulantly back into the pot.

They were silent a moment, just looking at each other, then they both started to laugh.

Wiping her eyes, Lisa turned to look at the pot on the stove. "Well, what should I do with this crap?" She peered into the pot. "We could add the green pepper like the recipe said, but I don't think it will improve things much."

Jack put his arms around her waist, leaning into her back and resting his chin on her head. "I think we need to keep plugging away on this cooking thing. I'm sure we'll both improve." He kissed the top of her head. "But maybe for tonight we should just bag the whole thing and go out for pizza."

"Yeah, that's a good idea. There's a new place on 52nd street that's supposed to be really good."

"The U district? We can hardly afford the gas to get there."

Lisa turned around in the circle of his arms to look at him. She frowned. "Jack, I've been thinking about this. I'm going to take my dad up on his offer. We could use some extra money until we get more on our feet. I'm tired of being so poor."

"But I thought we agreed to live within our means."

"Yeah, well, it was kind of fun at first, making do. But it's getting to be kind of a drag, and my folks have plenty of money."

"Let's save that option in case we get in a really bad spot. We both should be getting raises in the next six months or so. It'll get better."

"Yeah, sure, it'll get better. Kind of like our cooking, huh?"

He gave a low chuckle.

They had been living together a little more than a year when Lisa brought up the subject of marriage.

Surprised, Jack, who was sitting at the table grading papers, looked up at where Lisa was standing at the other side of the table leaning her elbows against the scarred surface. "You want to get married?" he said incredulously. "But I thought you didn't believe in marriage."

Lisa reached across the table to pick up the mug sitting by Jack's right hand and took a sip. "Your coffee's getting cold," she declared.

Jack raised an eyebrow.

Lisa set the cup back on the table. "It's true that I don't buy in to the traditional beliefs about marriage, but I was thinking that well, okay, here's a way to tell the whole world that I love you. And our folks would just eat it up."

Jack nodded. "My mom would be over the moon."

Lisa reached for his cup again, grimacing after she took another sip. "You definitely need to warm this up." She set the cup back down. "I'm not thinking about some kind of stuffy conventional ceremony. I won't promise to love, honor and obey. Well, love and honor work for me, that should be mutual. But obey? Not on your life."

Jack laughed, and standing up, pulled her to him.

33

Jack put another log on the fire, watching the flames fly up, then took a deep pull off his bottle of beer. He'd been here for hours, drinking beer and watching the flames, slouched low in the old velvet chair they'd had so much fun buying together at a secondhand store. Next to him was Lisa's favorite chair, a worn wooden rocker that her grandmother had given her when she and Jack had bought this little house a few years after they were married.

The chair was empty.

Their dog Phoebe, lying prone on the floor between the two chairs, looked up at him with questioning eyes, and he reached down to pat her head, trying to give her the reassurance he didn't feel.

Lisa was late. Based on past experience, Jack figured that she probably wouldn't come home tonight, wouldn't call. She had been to a three-day teacher's conference in Yakima and had said she'd be home at seven at the latest, in time for a late dinner together. It was now, he looked at his watch, after one-thirty in the morning.

Jack frowned. He was still willing to give her the benefit of the doubt despite his growing outrage at her lack of consideration. (What if she'd had a car accident? What if that was the reason why she was so late and not the usual shit?) Even now, when he was getting more and more angry with her, he knew he would welcome the *thunk* of her car door and the turn of the doorknob, her voice saying, "Jack? Jack? God, I'm sorry I'm so late," setting her bag down and her heavy purse, coming to hug him. Yes, even now he'd be willing to set his anger aside to say in a tired, patient voice, "That's okay—I was both worried sick and starting to get mad, but you're here now, and that's all that really matters. How did the conference go?"

But it was one-thirty. He looked at his watch, no, one-forty and still he was listening for her car and she wasn't here.

Behind him—he didn't turn to look but he could sense them sitting on the scarf Lisa had draped across the table— were the flowers that he'd picked in celebration of her home-coming. He imagined them wilting, drooping on their delicate stems over the side of the vase, stale and forgotten. The joy of finding them peeking through the tangle of their haphazardly weeded garden now faded. The chicken he had thawed was sitting unopened in the refrigerator and the marinade he had put together from a cookbook recipe was languishing in a bowl on the counter.

Tomorrow she'd call saying she had stopped for a drink with a colleague and they got into this great discussion and, "Well, you know how I am Jack, I just can't let a good argument go." Jack envisioned the rest of the scene. A fascinating subject, an interesting man who thought she was beautiful—so beautiful. He smiled ruefully. No, she wouldn't tell that part of the story.

And tomorrow she'd call, frantic in her desire for him to understand. She'd say, "Listen, Jack, I'm so sorry. You know that I love you so dearly. You're the best thing that ever happened to me and I never want to hurt you. It's just, you know how I am. I just don't think sometimes. Please, please forgive me."

She'd want him to forgive her, to make her feel better, and through the deep ache in his chest followed by the sarcasm, the accusations, the mutual pleas for understanding, the silences, he'd eventually say, "Yes, it's okay, I forgive you, I'm still here."

He patted Phoebe on the head again and she moved it to one side to capture his caress. He turned in his chair to look at the flowers. Well, okay, so they didn't look so bad after all, just sad—their purpose, the intent to please Lisa, unfulfilled.

He settled back in his chair, noticing that he was still listening, alert for the sound of the car door and her heavy tread up the front walk. Even now when it was what? Two o'clock, when he knew that she wouldn't be coming home tonight, he waited.

Jack shook the beer bottle. Almost empty. He knew that the last bit would be warm and bitter and he thought about dumping it out before he tipped it to his lips to get the last drops. He set the bottle on the floor next to his chair and watched the flames, still waiting.

He woke when Phoebe stirred beside him. She stood up and seconds later he heard the key turn and the slow creak of the door opening, followed by Lisa's quiet steps and the low murmur of her greeting to Phoebe.

He stood and turned to look. Lisa raised her head from where she was bending to pet Phoebe and said, "Jack."

"What?" he said, blinking. He ran his hand through his mussed hair.

"I'm really sorry."

He looked at his watch. It was 5:38 in the morning. "You're really late. You must have driven the whole way in the dark." When she nodded, he said, "That wasn't very safe." Still too groggy to feel much of anything, he looked at the woman before him. He knew it was Lisa, but she didn't seem real.

She was silent until he asked, "What happened?"

"A group of us stopped for a beer after the conference. We started talking about Reagan—you know, the cuts he's made to social services, his comments about homeless people—and it was starting to get late." She looked down at Phoebe, who was leaning against her leg, and scratched her behind an ear. "I was going to call, but somebody got to the phone before me, and when I tried later it was the same thing, and, I don't know, the time just got away from me."

"You realize, don't you, that you're something like ten hours late."

"Well, yes, but seven o'clock was just a ballpark time. You know what a long drive it is."

Jack just looked at her, trying to hold in his rising anger. "What changed your mind? I mean, what made you decide to come home? You weren't going to, were you?"

"I don't know, there were only a few of us left at the bar and it was getting late."

"Just two of you might be more accurate, right?"

Lisa didn't try to argue as she continued, "And I realized I just wasn't all that into the whole thing. I started to really miss this." She looked around her. "My husband, our home, our dog."

"Bully for you," Jack said, his voice flat.

"Yeah, well, you have every right to say that." She gave him a sad smile. "I screwed up."

"No shit."

"But I'm here now, and I think . . . I think I'm over that kind of thing, that kind of scene, hanging out late night at a bar." She set her purse on the table. "Oh! These flowers are lovely!"

"They were for our dinner together. I was going to try a new chicken marinade. Remember the dinner we had planned? You should have at least called."

She rubbed her eyes. "Jesus, Jack, I'm so sorry. I'm really, really sorry. It was a crappy thing to do."

Even though Jack was still too angry to acknowledge her apology, he felt his shoulders soften, the tension in his gut relax. He reached over to get Phoebe's leash off the hook by the door. "I'm taking Phoebe for a walk," he said.

"I'll come with you."

He hesitated before saying, "Okay."

As they walked down the sidewalk together, Phoebe trotting in front of them in the pre-dawn light, Lisa reached over and took his hand. He let her, even though he hadn't really forgiven her yet.

At a vacant lot two blocks down Jack unhooked Phoebe's leash to let her run. He and Lisa watched in amused silence as she ran to a tree to sniff its base, then ran to the next to sniff it in turn, then bounded off into the high grass, her joy apparent in the loll of her tongue and the dance in her steps.

Jack shivered in the chill air and Lisa leaned against him to lend him warmth. "You should have grabbed a coat," she told him.

"Yeah, that would've been smart," he said, shoving his hands deep into his pockets.

She linked her arm into his and leaned closer. "You know what? I've been thinking about the small bedroom."

"Oh. Yeah, I guess I need to clean up in there." He glanced at Lisa, who was gazing off into the distance. "Did you want to do anything special with it? Now that I'm done with grad school, I don't need to use it so much."

Lisa rubbed her nose to cover her smile. "I was thinking it

would make a good nursery." She felt the jerk of surprise that went through Jack's arm. "I'll be thirty before you know it and I'm thinking if we're going to have kids we should get started."

Jack drew apart enough to lean over and get a good look into her face. "Lisa, you're crazy," he told her.

She chuckled. "What else is new?" She waited a moment, then asked, "So, what do you think?"

Jack's voice was terse. "I think that a kid would have a hard time with a mom who is gone all night without explanation and a dad who is sick with worry."

"I told you I was done with that."

"How can I trust that? You've said the same thing before."

"Come on, Jack, you know that when I put my mind to something, that's what I do. I will be an excellent mom."

"But you always said you didn't want to bring a child into this world. The pollution, the overpopulation, war."

"Greed, exploitation, racism, sexism. I know, but I also think that there are things that make life worth living." She nodded toward Phoebe, who was attacking a weed with great enthusiasm. "Look at Phoebe. She's running around in a scrubby vacant lot in a neighborhood of shabby, tired looking houses. Nothing particularly special about it. And yet, right now, at this point in time, it's the most wonderful place on earth. Phoebe sees the beauty of each blade of grass and each tree and it fills her with joy."

Jack glanced in surprise at his normally pragmatic wife. "I understand exactly what you mean. It doesn't take much to make her happy." He smiled softly. "Kids are the same way. You know, when I was a boy, there was a dip at the end of our gravel driveway that would fill with water during a heavy rain, making the biggest, coolest mud puddle that was so much fun to stomp through on our way to school. There were a few times when the mud puddle had this beautiful undulating pattern floating on its surface, all different colors: green, blue, rust and purple. I remember the awe I felt when I saw that. It was so amazing and beautiful." He looked at Lisa, who tipped her head in question.

"What was it?'" she asked.

"Motor oil. One day when Steve and I were crouched over looking at it together this older boy came by and said, 'It looks like your old man's car has an oil leak. He better get that fixed before it ruins his motor.'"

Lisa grimaced in disgust. "Gross. Pollution."

"But we didn't know that. We thought it was beautiful." He toed a clump of dirt and watched with interest as the fragments rolled apart. "And you know what?"

"What?"

"It didn't change our perception of it as beautiful to know that it was only motor oil. We were kids. The whole world was beautiful to us. So sharp, vibrant and alive."

"So, what's your point, Jack?"

"Well, it's kind of like what you were saying about Phoebe and the vacant lot. This world isn't perfect, far from it. But it still has the capacity to bring joy." He looked at her and removed his arm from hers to encircle her waist. "So anyway, do I want to have kids? Yes. Because even though I know I can't protect them from the ugliness of life, I would still want to be able to share the sheer wonder of the discovery of beauty."

They turned to look at Phoebe who was down on her belly now, watching something they couldn't quite see. A bug, maybe? One thing for certain was that whatever it was that had her attention, it was, at this moment in time, the very best of its kind, the most amazing, wonderful thing in the whole world.

It was during the good times, the sweet, close days in the months that followed that Lisa became pregnant with Nathan. When she told him, Jack was overwhelmed with a sense of wonder. Everything looked different to him, brighter. Reminding himself that he was neither the first nor the last man to have a child didn't change the intensity of his joy. He was happy, he was scared, he was in love, both with Lisa and the child to come. He stopped off on the way home from work to buy a stuffed panda, leafed through family photo albums to see baby pictures, and looked more closely at his brother's baby daughter, marveling at her perfection.

Lisa's pregnancy was not a difficult one, morning sickness was minimal, and she woke up happy and full of energy more days than not. They both enjoyed watching the evolution of her belly from its usual robust roundness to the taut watermelon that thrummed with life. She invited him to rest his face against her abdomen to feel the baby's movements against his cheek, a bony elbow or the soft sole of a foot moving in a slow arc across the expanse of her round middle.

Jack thought he'd never seen her so content, and he'd never felt so completely loved. During the summer months before Nathan was born, Jack, who was on vacation and Lisa, who had taken an extended maternity leave, spent slow dreamy hours together, lounging in bed during the mornings, hand in hand, awaiting in awe this change that was coming to them, this amazing experience, this birth.

34

POULSBO, WASHINGTON, 1986

JACK, WITH three-year old Nathan in tow, trailed behind his very pregnant wife and the real estate agent. As he watched Lisa move in front of him, a sway from side to side added to her familiar determined tread, he noticed, and not for the first time, how she resembled some kind of ancient fertility figure when she was pregnant. Her breasts were overlarge, and the weight she had gained during her first pregnancy had expanded her thighs and bottom. Add to that her round middle and her short legs and the effect was similar to carvings he had seen depicting an ancient artisan's impression of a woman at the peak of potency. She wasn't altogether unattractive, he thought, but the exaggeration that pregnancy brought to her figure made her look like a caricature of a woman, not quite real.

He smiled. Lisa embraced pregnancy like she did everything else in life: at full volume, acting as though if she hadn't exactly invented it she at the very least had improved on it. Jack shook his head, bemused at his own thoughts and hefted Nathan to his shoulder as the real estate agent led them to some stairs on the outside of the two-car garage.

"I think you might find this especially tempting, Mrs. Wallace."

"McAffrey."

"Pardon me?"

"McAffrey. Ms. McAffrey. I kept my own name. Call me Lisa if that's more comfortable for you."

The realtor regarded Lisa, his eyes reassessing this matronly woman in the long purple dress, patterned scarf and leather sandals. "Certainly, Lisa, and as I was saying there is a bonus feature to this house." He opened the door and let Lisa and Jack pass into the tiny studio apartment. Jack set Nathan down on the oatmeal-colored rug and the little boy began to run in circles around the room. "Look, mommy and daddy! It's a whole little house! There's a stove and little 'frigerator, and look! There's the bathroom!"

Lisa caught Jack's eye. "Are you thinking what I'm thinking?"

"Marcie!" he said as the grin spread across his face.

"Exactly. She's been telling Mom that she wants a place of her own. This would be perfect for her!"

Jack turned to the real estate agent. "I think you may have just made a sale."

Two years later, checking on rosy-cheeked Stephen in the room they had decorated as a nursery, Jack smoothed his son's blond hair, damp and tousled from sleep. He made certain that the rail to the crib was locked firmly in place. Stephen, at eighteen months, was starting to crawl out of his crib. They really needed to get him a toddler bed soon. Jack turned as Lisa entered the room. "How's Nathan?" he asked.

"Nathan's all snuggled in and starting to drift off," Lisa said as she tucked the blanket more firmly around the sleeping Stephen.

She lifted her gaze to Jack, who was rubbing at a spot on the front of his shirt, wondering if it was something from the kid's dinner.

Through the open door they heard Marcie in the kitchen, saying, "Now, this here is Stephen's tippy cup. He can't have a regular cup yet because he spills. Nathan uses this cup usually. See? It's plastic in case he drops it."

Smiling, Lisa closed the door. "Marcie's in the kitchen showing your mom around so she knows where everything is." She shook her head. "Marcie's pretty proud of her apartment and her arrangement with us. She considers the whole place her personal domain, I think."

"Yeah, she's taken on quite the Lady of The Manor role!"

Lisa chuckled. "It's a totally different role for her to play hostess and she's playing it to the hilt. Pretty cool." Her voice shifted, serious now. "So anyway, I showed your mom our emergency number list and she has the Rubinstein's number in case she needs to reach us, so I guess we're all set."

"Okay," Jack said. "And don't worry about Mom. She's raised a couple of boys of her own, you know." He hesitated. "Is that a new shirt you're wearing? It looks really good on you."

"It's one of my new blouses, size gargantuan," Lisa told him as she smoothed the front of the multicolored blouse, an import from Guatemala. "The one I was going to wear was too tight." Lisa frowned. "God, Jack, I've put on so much weight!" she mourned.

Jack knew better than to try and contradict her. She would call him on it. "But you're still my lovely Lisa," he said, then smiled playfully. "The voluptuous conquering Valkyrie, woman of my dreams."

"Thanks Jack, but I don't think anyone else would agree with you on that."

"Nonsense!" He put his arms around her waist, much wider

these days, but still nice to hold, then seductively ran his hands down her hips. He actually kind of liked the extra pounds she'd put on. She had become softer, more womanly, but she wouldn't want to hear that, so he kept it to himself. He added an exaggerated bump and grind to make her smile.

Laughing, Lisa let him hold her for a few moments before pulling away.

"Did you check Stephen's diaper?" she asked.

"All ship shape, me captain!" he quipped.

Never satisfied that anyone could parent as well as she could, Lisa hooked a finger under the edge of Stephen's diaper to check for dampness. Jack didn't mind; it was Lisa's nature to always want to be in charge, and that was no reflection on her confidence in him.

A curly tendril fell across her rounded cheek as she gave Stephen's bottom a loving pat. Jack watched her, thinking that she'd kept her vow, made when they first discussed having children, to tone herself down enough to be a good mother. And of course, she wasn't just a good mother, she was an excellent one.

Well, mostly.

It had been less than a year ago, hadn't it, when she'd called him from the police station.

"They arrested me for civil disobedience, Jack!" she had told him. Over the phone her voice sounded different, distant. "Can you fucking believe that?"

Actually, he did. Running his fingers through his hair, Jack had sighed before saying, "Lisa, didn't we talk about you taking a back seat at the demonstration? I mean, we agreed that because you were taking the boys you would play it safe." He became silent. The boys. If she was in jail, where were their kids? He tuned back into Lisa, who was saying, "Yeah, I was playing it cool, I really was, Jack, but then the cop told us to move back, and there was no reason we should have to do that! We had every right to be there!"

"Where are the kids?"

"What? Oh, the kids. I had to tell the cop that Maria, who been standing next to me the whole time, was my sister so she could take them."

"Who the hell is Maria?" Jack realized that he'd shouted it, but he didn't care. His kids were with a stranger.

"She's cool, Jack, she's one of us. Calm down. She has them here at the station. I need you to come and bail me out."

The kids were all right. Maria, who Lisa had just met that day, was reading them a book when Jack arrived at the station.

Driving Lisa and the boys home, he had little to say. He had put up with a lot from Lisa, but he drew the line at putting their kids in danger. That night he made himself a bed on the couch. He had nothing to say to Lisa. He didn't even want to look at her.

She didn't apologize. Of course. But she did her best to show him that she wouldn't do anything to endanger their kids again, and, as always, Jack forgave her.

Feeling a flash of anger, he jerked back from the memory. It still had the power to goad him, and that wasn't what he wanted tonight. Tonight, they were going to let things go and enjoy themselves.

"See you around ten or eleven," Lisa was telling his Mom as she and Jack moved to the door, and she assured them that it was no problem. "Just go and have fun. Don't worry about the time."

As Lisa put on her coat, Jack's eyes rested fondly on her high cheekbones and soft, full lips. His thoughts returned to her complaints about the extra pounds she had put on. Even overweight Lisa was still capable of turning heads. And yet, it seemed as though motherhood had leeched out her tendency toward sidelong glances and knowing smiles that he'd been tortured by all these years. Thank God, because he was so weary of the ups and downs that came with that. He watched her pull out the thick tendrils that had been caught under the collar of her coat, the uniformity of her dark curls now broken by an occasional gray hair.

Lisa pulled open the door, not waiting for him to hold it for her, and strode on her short legs across the lawn to the car. She was such a vibrant person, passionate and vocal about social justice, forever the champion of the disenfranchised people of the world, her voice raised and her eyes flashing, so sure in her opinions and ready to argue with anyone with a dissenting view. He admired her for that even if her blind dedication caused some friction between them now and again.

She really wasn't altogether easy to live with, to tell the truth, but it only took one of her smiles for him to feel the wash of love that came over him so easily. He slid his arm into the sleeve of his jacket, then settled it around his shoulders. That love was always there, even when he was cross with her over her latest impulsive choice to give half her paycheck to a defense fund or cancel long-anticipated weekend plans to attend a march.

Jack closed the door behind him and followed Lisa across the yard, noticing how her long coat swayed about her calves as she walked. In the sparse light of the evening, the big coat made her look like a bear from the back. Truly a formidable foe to anyone who was naive enough to oppose her.

Watching the figure in front of him, he thought, yes, she really had put on a good deal of weight, but what the hell, he was getting a bit worn around the edges himself. This softer, rounder version of Lisa seemed more settled, happier, if just a bit over the top in her opinions about child rearing, which after all (he smiled at this) would be normal for Lisa.

Overtaking her on the path, Jack slowed Lisa's forward progress down enough to put his arm through hers. She leaned lightly against him and nuzzled his neck and for a short moment life felt orderly, just right. At least for now, and that was good enough for him. For certain there would be some tough times ahead, he knew that, but he also knew that they would manage together to do this, this whole marriage and parenting thing, and do it well.

35

Kitsap Peninsula, Spring 2009

Jack strode through the parking lot, shirt sleeves rolled up, the rumpled tails untucked from his jeans, blazer swinging lightly in one hand. Cottonwood fluff drifted around him and the air had the delicate smell of early flowers. Spring at last! And a Friday afternoon with good news to bring home to Lisa, he thought in elation.

His smile wavered. She'd been sick lately, was going through tests to rule out cancer. But no, it was nothing, he was sure. How could she be sick? She was a strong woman. She simply wouldn't allow it. Especially with spring coming on and everything feeling so fresh and new. He flopped his blazer onto the hood of his car as he fished out his keys.

He turned as his friend David, his usual baggy corduroy pants, too warm for this weather, belt riding low under a protruding belly, sauntered up to the car. "Hey Jack, I hear that you got the okay to add the children's lit class to the curriculum. So what's on the syllabus, 'Green Eggs and Ham?'"

Jack ignored David's ribbing. "I hadn't really considered Dr. Seuss for the reading list, but that's a possibility. 'The Bitter Butter Battle Book' is kind of interesting." He smiled. "I remember reading that one to my boys when they were little. Wow. That was more than twenty years ago. Hard to believe they're all grown up."

"Anyway," he said, pulling his attention back to the subject at hand, "I'm looking at classical children's literature, chapter books like 'Treasure Island,' 'Wind in the Willows' and 'Little Women.' Ones that people of all ages can enjoy." Jack leaned against the car door, his keys in the lock temporarily forgotten. "It seems like children's literature is a genre that is so often overlooked and yet so important. Those stories are part of what forms us, what moves us toward certain choices later in life, you know? I mean, for example, who are you?"

David shrugged, not sure whether the question was rhetorical as Jack pressed on,

"Are you like Ratty, drifting contentedly on the river, or are you like Toad, who is never satisfied? Are there people in your life who are manipulative and duplicitous like Long John Silver? Have you experienced loss like Jo in 'Little Women' and found that you could survive it?"

Jack, hearing his own words, noticed with joy that he was actually feeling passionate about this course. It was like he had woken up again after the last few dusty years of teaching when he had found himself less than enthusiastic about his work. At last! he thought. I'm coming back to life, regaining my old excitement over the process of teaching. This class was going to be great. Suddenly he was eager to be home, wished there wasn't a half-hour drive between here and home. Lisa would be so happy for him—he couldn't wait to see her. The spike of worry came back as he remembered that she was waiting for test results. Oh, but it would be fine.

Jack looked at David who had stood silent during Jack's discourse but now looked ready to add his own thoughts. No time for that; Jack just wanted to get home. "Good to see you,

David. I've really gotta go. Thanks for listening to me drone on. We'll talk later." Jack opened his car door, slipped into the seat and drove a little too fast out of the parking lot, leaving David behind, his face lined with consternation.

During the drive home Jack thought about "The Wind in the Willows." Which of the characters was most like Lisa? Badger? It had been awhile since he'd read the book, but he remembered Badger as a strong character, authoritative. She'd probably see herself as most like Badger, but really, wasn't she a bit like Toad, always running after the newest thing? But not shallow like Toad. He frowned, suddenly realizing that all the characters in "The Wind in the Willows" were male. The same was true of another book he was considering for the class, "Winnie the Pooh"—with the exception of the kangaroo. All white for that matter, too. Sure, they were animal characters, but the implication was that if they were human they'd be white. And upper class. He frowned. He needed to dig deeper, find some books that offered some diversity. "Little Women" had strong female characters, but again, they were all white people. Hmm, good topic for discussion, that. The push for white male supremacy carried out in children's books and how that influences us psychologically. What were the implications for little girls and children of color? He smiled. This was going to be a great topic to discuss with Lisa over dinner tonight. She would definitely have a lot to say. He imagined the heat coming to her cheeks as she would dig into the topic, ranting about the effect of white male privilege on the developing minds of children.

He turned onto his street. Only a few blocks to go and he would be home.

He felt it before he even opened the door. Sunny was in the yard and she greeted him quietly, her tail wagging softly. He patted her head. "What's up, old girl? Why so gloomy?"

When he opened the door he was aware right away of Lisa's voice coming from the kitchen, the tone low and quiet, not like Lisa at all. Something was wrong—he felt it in his gut. His feet were too big, too heavy as he moved toward her. He was aware of the sound of his own unsteady breath.

She sat at the kitchen table with her back half turned to him, her shoulders hunched. No, that wasn't her. Lisa didn't sit like that, huddled like a crow embattled by the wind. She turned and gave him a little wave. It *was* her. But it was not, couldn't be.

The sun from the window fell full on her hair and he noticed how the gray that wove through the strands picked up the light in sharp contrast to the dark. He saw dust motes floating in the stream of sunlight, so unreal. And the voice that was hers and not hers was speaking softly into the phone. It reminded him of the tone she reserved for the kids when they were small, patient and gentle.

"That's all I know for now, Stephen. I'll tell you when I have more news."

Jack watched her wipe a tear from her cheek and then look at it, puzzled. "No, that's okay, honey, don't come up—you have your job, and it's such a long drive. I'll let you know if I need you." She was silent for a moment, listening. She glanced briefly at Jack then lowered her eyes. "Yes, I know. Me too. But whatever happens it's going to be okay. I love you, Stephen. Please give my love to Sandy."

She put the phone down and looked up at Jack, nodding her head toward the chair opposite her so that he would sit down.

"You got the test results," he said flatly, fighting the fear in his gut.

"It's not good, Jack."

"Oh God, Lisa, it's cancer?"

"Liver."

"Isn't that . . . I mean, it's one of the bad ones, isn't it?" He willed her to tell him that it wasn't true.

"The survival rate at this point in time is only about eleven percent. If I'd gone in when I should have it might have been better, but you know how it is. I was too busy to pay attention to minor details like pain that was like a fist in my side. I kept thinking it would go away." This was said almost as an apology as she looked at Jack, her expression of unreality mirroring his own.

"God, babe, I didn't know . . ."

"That's because I didn't tell you."

Jack felt uncomfortable in his skin, wanted to remove himself from it, to not be here, to be the Jack who was so elated not even an hour ago. He made himself stay present, knew that she needed him here. He scooted his chair close to hers and reached out his arms. She stood and pulled him to his feet so that they could hold each other close, belly to belly, chest to chest, their sobs blending into one, a single wail of loss.

36

Poulsbo, Washington, November 2013

There was a certainty of change within her, reverberating through Raymie like a drumbeat. Dinner at Jack and Marcie's house was a date, even though the word had not been spoken.

Fingers clumsy with excitement, Raymie dressed in the kind of clothing she loved, suspecting that Jack would appreciate her taste: a white blouse with billowy sleeves, a black embroidered vest, faded blue jeans and short boots with a small heel. It was a fun outfit, a pirate's garb, but pretty.

The things she planned to take neatly gathered together, Raymie realized there was still a good half-hour before Jack and Marcie would show. Not sure what to do with herself in the interim, she leaned against the little table in the hallway and called Shainy over to play catch, throwing the ball without noticing what she was doing, tense and restless, one of her legs jiggling like crazy of its own accord.

A little before five-thirty there was the expected knock on the door. Raymie opened it to Jack, who had come to pick her up by himself this time, looking almost forlorn under the glow of her porch light, hands shoved in his pockets and arms pressed close to his sides.

"Please come in!" Raymie told him. "You must be freezing out there! I won't be but a minute."

As he made to take off his boots, she added, "Oh, no. Don't worry about that, there's plenty of dirt in here from Shainy and me."

He wiped his boots on the doormat, doing quite a job of it, probably feeling awkward, Raymie thought, without the gregarious Marcie at his side. She watched, aware of the scrape of his boots on the fiber doormat, the curve of his neck, the heavy folds of his coat. She caught the scent of fresh shampoo from his bent head, basic and good.

Jack looked up, eyes catching hers, then walked in the door, closing it behind him. Thrown off balance by his nearness, Raymie stepped back to create a more comfortable distance between them.

Jack helped restore the equilibrium by conjuring up the image of Marcie bustling about the kitchen at their house. "Marcie told me to go ahead without her. She was holding down the fort, industriously chopping vegetables when I left. She wouldn't hear of being interrupted."

Raymie smiled and nodded. "Marcie told me that you were cooking chicken tonight." She looked at the bag she had set by the door. "I got some white wine to go with it. Is Chardonnay all right?"

"Chardonnay is great."

"And some diet soda for Marcie, although she told me that she will take a small glass of wine now and again."

"She might take a little, but I think she prefers the sweet stuff." Seeming to detect disappointment in Raymie's face, he added, "Can't stand the stuff myself. I prefer a dry wine like Chardonnay."

Jack offered to carry the bag with the wine and soda and they walked to his car, Shainy trotting happily ahead, most likely anticipating some play time with Shep.

At the house they found Marcie in the kitchen, which was cozy-warm and smelled marvelous, with her kitten, already much bigger than when Raymie last saw her, twining herself around Marcie's legs, and Shep standing in the doorway with his tail wagging. "Hi Rainy!" Marcie said, putting down a stirring spoon to wrap her in a big hug and then bending to pat Shainy on the head. "Hi there, Shainy!"

Jack put the bag on the counter. "I'll take over from here, Marcie."

Marcie took off the chef's apron and handed it to Jack with a bow of mock ceremony. "Jack's making white sauce," she said, turning to Raymie. "He makes it really good. I tried to make it myself once but it came out all goopy and lumpy." She wrinkled her nose. "Gumpy," she said, then laughed.

"Please make yourself comfortable," Jack said as he pulled something—Raymie thought it might be a wire whisk—from a drawer next to the stove. "Can we offer you anything?"

"I could open the wine."

"Oh, of course. Let me get you an opener. Marcie? Do you want some wine too?"

Jack moved aside to let Raymie wash her hands at the kitchen sink, the closeness of his body both reassuring and arousing, a strange combination that, oddly, seemed to calm her, to put her at ease. Raymie started to open the wine, twisting the corkscrew as she held the green neck of the bottle, then hesitated. "I can pour for us, but I have to put a finger at the rim of the glass to feel when it's full. Would that bother either of you?

"Oh, you can put your fingers in my glass any time," Jack quipped, then looked startled at what he had just said.

The room was still for a moment. Marcie, who was nuzzling the kitten, set her down on the floor before saying, "Oh, Jack, you say the weirdest things sometimes!"

"Sorry," Jack said with a little grimace. "That didn't come out quite the way I meant it to."

Blushing with pleasure, Raymie shrugged to let him know it was no big deal and then poured Marcie a glass of wine. Marcie took a sip before saying, "Yish!" and trading it in for her usual soda. Raymie took Marcie's glass for herself and poured one for Jack.

Jack took small sips of his wine, giving a nod of approval at the taste, while he made the white sauce, looking comfortable among the pots and pans of his kitchen. Raymie took a seat at the table and Shainy, who had been sitting patiently, looked at her in expectation. "Yes, go play." As soon as Shainy stood up, Shep bounced forward and they started romping around in the middle of the room. Marcie leaned toward them and pointed a finger toward the living room. "Hey, you two! Take your roughhousing someplace else," she commanded, then got some UNO cards out of a cupboard. "Let's play a couple of games while we wait for dinner."

Mid-way through the game, Marcie triumphantly slapped down a Draw Four. "Hah!" she said. "I got you now, you scurvy dog!"

Raymie laughed in surprise.

"We've developed quite a repertoire of game-related insults and comebacks over the years," Jack said. Raymie turned to see him leaning against the counter, the chef's apron now balled up in his hand. "Your retort might be, 'Nothing can slow me down, you slimy snake in the grass!'"

Raymie laughed again, enjoying the smile he gave her in

return. Then he said, "Well, dinner's ready, for what it's worth. It's an old recipe but I never know exactly how it will turn out. And Marcie made the salad. She always comes up with something new, so I'm sure that will be good."

"It smells wonderful, Jack! And Marcie, you are a woman after me own heart. I love a good salad."

Raymie gathered up the cards while Marcie set the table. Jack, checked mitts on his hands, presented them with a beautiful chicken and vegetable dish with a creamy white sauce.

They all scooted up to the table, politely passing the dishes to one another and buttering the crusty bread that Jack had added as a finishing touch.

"You should taste his Thanksgiving turkey!" Marcie told Raymie when she complemented Jack's cooking. She tipped her head. "You're coming to our house for Thanksgiving, aren't you, Raymie?"

Jack looked up from his plate, surprised.

"I usually spend Thanksgiving with my daughter," Raymie said.

"She can come too!"

Jack smiled apologetically. "Marcie really likes you."

"Damn right I do," Marcie declared. "And you like her too."

"Yes, I like her too," Jack said softly, head ducked as he poked around at his food.

"Oh, but I wouldn't want to impose. It would mean four extra people at the table."

"Alright! We can put an extra leaf in the big table, Jack!"

Jack looked up. "Would you and your daughter and . . ."

"My son-in-law and my grandson."

"Would the four of you like to join us for Thanksgiving dinner? I can't promise much—it's a fairly small gathering, just Marcie, and me, and my sons and their . . . partners, and their kids. That's eight, plus the four of you. Actually. I guess it wouldn't be all that small."

"Are you sure that you can accommodate the extra people?"

"Absolutely," Jack said.

"Absolutamently!" Marcie added, grinning.

"Absolutomently?"

"It's a word in the same class as gumpy," Jack offered. "A Marcie-ism."

"I think I rather like Marcie-isms."

After dinner they cleared the table to prepare for another game of UNO. Before beginning to deal the cards, Jack got something from the top of the refrigerator and handed it to Raymie, a small sheaf of papers. As Raymie peered at them, he said, "The last time you were over you had asked to see some of my poems. These are mostly old, but there are also a few new ones. I wrote them in extra-large print. Will that work for you?"

"Oh, yes, I can read these! Thank you."

Marcie leaned over the table and took one of the poems from near the bottom of the pile. "This one has your name in it, Rainy. Look, it's called Sweet Rain."

"A poem about rain? How lovely." Raymie passed the poem to Jack. "Jack, will you read it? I love to hear a poem read aloud by the poet. You know best how you want it to sound."

Jack took the poem, but seemed uncertain. "Wouldn't you like to hear one of the others first?"

"Oh, let's hear this one first, Jack," Marcie urged. "This is the one you wrote a couple of weeks ago, huh?"

They both looked at him expectantly.

"Okay, well, it's a poem about the five senses. I actually think it came out pretty well."

He settled against the kitchen counter and pulled a pair of reading glasses from his shirt pocket. He was silent for a moment and then began to read. His voice held the hypnotic rhythm of someone who was well practiced in reading poetry.

In shades of gray
the arc of day
Illuminates the rainy world.

Her textured hand
surveys the land, delighted
by the dips and whorls.

And to her sense
the eloquence
of living flavors blend.

Sea bird's cry
cedar's sigh
whisper whoosh of wind.

Pungent smell of salty reef
fragrance of a dying leaf
scent of freshened sky.

All these things
the sweet rain brings
that I had thought gone by.

So many sensations, most of them physical, all happening at once. Raymie couldn't look at him. "That is so beautiful," she breathed, eyes on her folded hands. Jack's poem so aptly described the world as she sensed it. The heightened sounds, the eloquence of scent and touch, of taste, the faded colors, still so beautiful, so sensual.

Jack spoke and she turned her eyes to his. "Thank you," he said, and set the poem gently back on the pile. "Do you want to wait to read the others later? That one was probably the best of the group."

"Hey, yeah, let's get to playing our game," Marcie told them. "You can read the rest later. But before we start the game, I'm gunna have some more soda. Do you two want some more wine?"

"Thank you, Marcie, that would be really welcome right now," Raymie told her.

Caught in the stillness of anticipation, Raymie was quiet as Jack drove her back to her house. Marcie, sitting in the back with Shainy, provided a rambling monologue that gave her respite from the effort of trying to make normal conversation when the deeper words, the words of intimacy, were still unsaid.

Jack pulled up in front of Raymie's house and turned off the engine. She and Jack got out, and he opened one of the back doors for Shainy. Marcie, getting out just long enough to give Raymie a big hug, immediately got back into the car after an exaggerated "brrr!"

Raymie felt for Shainy's collar and snapped on her leash while Jack stood waiting. "No moon tonight," he said, "and I think that it's starting to ice up. I could walk with you, if you like."

The part of Raymie that would have protested that she

didn't need any help to walk to her own front door pressed forward, and she shooed it back. "Thank you, Jack, that would be good."

"Do you want to take my arm?"

Raymie reached out. She couldn't really see him in the dark, but sensed him as an area of warmth in the chilly air. He guided her hand to his elbow, her fingers making contact with the fabric of his coat. The rich smell of damp wool made her want to bury her nose in his shoulder to breathe it in.

As they moved down her front walk, Raymie was aware that it was cold, very cold, but she didn't feel it. Everything was ice, crystalline. Time was moving slowly, deliberate in its forward motion. Shainy walked carefully in front of them. Seeming to sense their mood, she stepped softly, patient and gentle.

When they reached the door, Raymie let her hand slip from Jack's arm. "Thank you," she said, attuned to the hush in her own voice. She stood there, remembering that the next thing would be to unlock the door. Feeling in the pocket of her coat, she ran her fingers over the keys nestling there.

"It was good to spend the evening with you, Rainy."

Raymie nodded. "I had a lovely time," she said. Then hesitating a moment, added, "I'm glad you've started calling me Rainy. I really like that name."

She could hear Jack's smile more than see it. "It's a good name. It really suits you." His voice then changing to a heartier tone, he said, "And it was good to see you again, Shainy." He bent down to pet her head.

As he stood up, Raymie put a hand softly on his arm. They were like that for a moment, just the sound of their breath in the cold, then he moved forward to kiss her on the cheek.

Raymie turned her mouth to meet his. The kiss was light,

careful. He drew apart to kiss her on the top of her head, her brow, the tip of her nose. Then, with a soft moan that might have come from either of them, his mouth again found hers.

37

November 2013, Thanksgiving

The turkey was just starting to brown, Raymie was finishing a salad and Marcie was sliding a dish of sweet potatoes into the oven when Jack left the kitchen to go to the apartment above the garage. He hated to leave this homey scene, but their guests would be coming soon and his faded t-shirt and stained jeans needed to go.

In the apartment Jack pulled on a clean pair of jeans and tucked in his shirt, a new one, still crisp to the touch even after its first wash. As he slid the tails into his jeans, he noticed the waistband was looser than he remembered, confirming his suspicion that he'd lost weight. He paused to smile. "It must be all the sex," he thought. "That Raymie! She . . ." No, he wouldn't think about that right now, the kids and grandkids would be coming soon and this wasn't the time to be thinking about that. And yet the memory pressed in of her hands running down his body, their sensitivity to each angle and curve.

Shaking his head, Jack sat down on the edge of the bed to put on his shoes and socks, noticing with wonder how alive his feet felt. He wiggled his toes. "Nice things, toes," he said to himself, then muttered, "Well, Jack, you're just a bit of a nutcase today, aren't you?"

He stood up. "Okay. Next step, shave." Jack walked over to

the bathroom and leaned over the sink to peer at himself in the medicine cabinet mirror. He sure was getting gray, that was for certain, but his mustache was still salt and pepper, unevenly so. Should he shave off his mustache? Not today, but later? He stroked the mustache thinking about the time he'd shaved it off and Lisa made it clear that she did not approve. But maybe Raymie wouldn't mind. He shrugged. Or maybe he liked his mustache and would just decide for himself.

The latch on the medicine cabinet made a nice snick as he opened it to get out the shaving cream and his razor. He set them on the ledge of the sink as he thought about who would be coming today. There would be Raymie's daughter Allison, who he'd never met, and Allison's son Aaron, a toddler that Raymie called the love of her life. Allison's husband, apparently, had begged off. Raymie said he was an asshole anyway and didn't care if he came or not. Did she say asshole? She rarely swore, so he wasn't sure, but that was the general idea.

Stephen had come up from Fresno with Sandy and their kids yesterday, and would be arriving from their hotel soon. And Nathan would be coming too, with his new partner, David, a surprise to them all, including Nathan himself. After a couple of disappointingly short relationships with really quite nice women, Nathan had finally found the right person to share his life. Jack had only met David once very briefly, but he remembered Nathan's tender pride, his love, as he looked at the younger man, and Jack felt satisfied that Nathan was happy in this relationship. Although—Jack frowned—he was still adjusting to the idea of having a gay son.

He chuckled fondly. Lisa, on the other hand, would have embraced Nathan's gayness with gusto and probably would have wanted to take part in events like the Pride Parade in

Seattle, whether Nathan chose to be a participant or not. "Hell, she'd have had a hand in organizing the thing," he muttered as he sprayed shaving cream into his palm. For Jack it just felt a little awkward still, having a gay son, different from what he was used to. Looking at his reflection in the mirror, he practiced introducing the couple to his friends: "This is my son Nathan and his partner David."

No, that sounded like they were in business together.

"Come on, Jack, man up," he told his reflection. "This is your son's boyfriend."

Man up? Really? Talk about an archaic phrase! Jack laughed, amused at himself.

He patted on the shaving cream. Things change. The changes he'd seen in his lifetime were nothing less than astounding. Truly astounding. His generation had broken new ground, brought about changes in social equality, and the next generations were continuing to push forward. It wasn't perfect, probably never would be given that they were human. There would be steps forward and plenty back. But his granddaughters would have more choices than women of his generation ever dreamed of, and his son Nathan was free to love who he wanted and do it openly, although Jack imagined that it wasn't always going to be easy.

As he ran the razor down his right cheek Jack marveled at the myriad changes in the human condition that had taken place over the centuries. An image came to mind from a drawing, or maybe it was a film, of the generations before him moving forward in a slow steady line, the physical form evolving over time, clothing changing, becoming more elaborate and richer in color. He imagined people walking singly and in pairs, holding the hands of their children, the children growing up, letting go, forming their own families, then growing old, dying away as new generations were born. And amid this came the emergence of the world's culture: art, religion, literature, and scientific inventions, innovations of every kind— new ideas, both profound and absurd.

Jack nodded to himself. Yes, that was all good, but you couldn't ignore that the counterpart to that progress, that forward movement of human cultural evolution, was the act of war, the tendency to cheat and steal, to murder out of jealousy and greed, to betray one another. "And let's not forget what we humans have done to the environment," Jack muttered, turning his face from side to side to check for nicks. Good. Not a bad job for once.

When they were first dating, Lisa had said to him, "It's crazy to even think about bringing children into this fucked-up world," yet she chose to have kids after all and raised their boys with such hope, so much love. Even she, who was acutely aware of injustice, of human waste and folly, thought the world was a place worth living in. He remembered her bending lovingly toward the boys, placing a kiss on the top of a head, a hand cupping a chubby cheek, and felt some sadness edging in. Lisa didn't have the opportunity to get to know her grandchildren. She would have loved them so much.

He tapped his razor on the sink and rinsed it, hearing the snick of the medicine cabinet as he opened it to put the razor away.

Returning to the image of the human march through time, Jack saw his place in that slowly moving line, how he'd found a wife, created a family, and now was growing old, would someday be gone, as the next generation reinvented the world as they needed to, making it their own.

Jack waited to feel some sadness about that, but didn't. He frowned. Sure, it would be hard to let go, to say, "Okay, it's your world now," but he knew he could—was already doing it, actually—and he hoped, with grace. After all, passing knowledge on to the next generation also required letting go, of having the faith that they can manage without you.

He regarded himself critically. Not bad for an old guy. Growing old is a unique experience, he thought, just like all the other life passages. It's kind of interesting to be able to stand back and notice the shifts in perspective as it changes with the years. And with that thought came a sudden surge of excitement, of curiosity about what would happen next, feelings that had been dormant in him for a long time now. It wasn't over yet, this walk through life. There was still more to come, and he was excited to be part of it.

To tell the truth, he didn't really feel that old. What was old? He was who he was. This was just his latest manifestation, this guy in the mirror with the unruly gray hair and the lines at the corners of his eyes.

Jack turned his head toward the hollow sound of someone coming up the stairs to the apartment. It was followed by a light knock on the door and the creak of hinges. "Jack?"

He switched off the bathroom light, stepped into the main room. And there she was, waiting for him. Raymie.

"Everyone will be arriving soon," Raymie said, and when she saw the sharp intake of his breath, asked, "Nervous?"

He nodded. "But mostly happy, Rainy my love. Mostly happy."

As they walked over to the house, he reached out to take her hand and noticed how that simple gesture felt both so wonderfully new and, at the same time, so completely ancient.

38

NATHAN SET A DISH of cranberry sauce in the middle of the table, a bony wrist poking out of the sleeve of his shirt as he turned it to sit more squarely in the center.

"How's it going?" he asked.

Allison glanced up from where she was bending over a place setting to meet his friendly gaze. His eyes were a rich dark brown as was his hair—his mother's coloring, she imagined—but he was a little gawky like his dad, tall and lanky. She had met Nathan and his boyfriend David when she arrived at the house, late as was usually the case with her (she mentally rolled her eyes) after getting lost on her way here.

She had liked the pair instantly, especially Nathan, and she had flirted with the idea of having him as a step-brother. She'd never had a brother; the closest she ever came was her cousin Matt, her uncle Keith's son, who was a lot younger than she and lived several states away. Nathan seemed like he would be the kind of brother you could tell things to. (A picture came to mind of her telling him what a jerk her husband was and him nodding in sympathy.) Yes, it would be nice to have a brother or two, she thought, as she smiled back at Nathan. She had also met Stephen, shorter, rounder and lighter haired, and found him very likable, although he seemed pretty absorbed in his career and the house he and his wife were building in California. Stephen and Sandy had two girls a little older than her son. Potential cousins. Or step-cousins actually—practically the same thing to a little kid. She noticed the longing that arose from the center of her chest. Yes, it would be nice.

"It's going pretty good, but I'm a little confused about where the napkin should go."

"Oh, you think I'd know that working in a restaurant," Nathan told her. "But different places do it differently. At home David and I tend to be pretty casual and don't pay a lot of attention to that kind of thing.'"

"We're pretty casual at my house too."

"Hey, I know! Mom used to have these napkin rings. Want me to look for them?" He stepped over to an old wooden buffet that looked like it might be a family heirloom and opened a drawer. "Here they are!" he said, handing her a small box. "Just slide one over a napkin and set it in the middle of the plate. Does that work for you?"

"Sure, that's great, makes it easy." Allison put a napkin ring that was bright with Southwestern colors over a napkin. "You're a chef, aren't you?"

"Actually, I'm a sous-chef. I'm next in line for the chef position when the present one steps down. If that ever happens in my lifetime, that is. The Metro Bistro is a really good restaurant," he explained, "so there's a lot of competition for jobs." He hesitated, noticing that he was running on a bit. "You should come check it out. Have you ever eaten there?"

"I've heard of it and I looked at their menu online. It all sounds fantastic, but I can't afford to eat there."

"Me neither," Nathan said, grinning at her. Allison returned his grin, and suddenly feeling shy turned back to setting the table.

"This looks really nice," Nathan told her. "It feels wonderful to have a large gathering for Thanksgiving again. After Mom died we were a pretty pathetic little group."

"Did you have a lot more family over when your mom was alive?"

"Yeah, well, grandparents sometimes when they lived closer, and my aunts and uncles sometimes, but I'm not sure how comfortable our extended family was with all the extra people Mom would invite."

"Extra people?"

"Mom seemed to invite people fairly randomly. You never knew who would show up. Like, people who were involved in one or another political group, or people who were homeless, stranded refugees, friends who were recently divorced and alone for the holiday and so on. It was fun, but it could get pretty chaotic." He straightened a corner of the tablecloth. "We got to hear a lot of political rhetoric, people soapboxing, if that's the correct word, about whatever they were passionate about. One time there was this guy who said that we shouldn't celebrate Thanksgiving because of all the wrongs done to the Native Americans. Of course he was right about that, so the next year we didn't have Thanksgiving at all, but because Mom loved hosting a big noisy gathering, the year after that we went back to our usual celebration." He laughed, shaking his head.

"Your mom must have been a wonderful person. A real mover and shaker, as they say."

"I could have done with a little less moving and shaking to tell you the truth, but all in all she was a really great mom."

"You miss her."

Nathan looked up. She could see the moisture in his eyes.

"Are you okay with my mom being here? I mean, with her

and your dad?"

"God yes! I haven't seen Dad so happy in a long time."

"She's a lot different from how your mom was."

"Yeah, she's not at all like Mom but I bet they would have liked each other. Aunt Marcie's a lot like Mom, and she and Raymie seem to get along famously."

"I'm quite taken with Marcie myself."

He laughed. "You and everybody else! She's quite the character."

He was silent a moment, smiling, his eyes soft with memories, then seemed to rouse himself. "Well, I'd better get back to the kitchen. I told Dad I'd help him slice the turkey." He gave her a little twisted smile. "Wish us luck. Dad can be a little scary with a carving knife, especially now that he has to wear reading glasses to do it. I wouldn't want him to mistake his finger for one of the wings or something."

Allison chuckled. "Mom said that he is kind of clumsy. I think she finds it very endearing."

"Kind of clumsy? That was very charitable of her. Sometimes he's downright dangerous!"

Allison was still laughing when he left the dining room.

When he walked into the kitchen Nathan felt a warm wash of love come over him. There was David, sleeves rolled up and decked out in a yellow and orange bib apron that had been Lisa's and that clashed harshly with his deep plum shirt, scooping mashed potatoes from a pan to a bowl, a lock of hair bobbing over his forehead as he bent to his task. Next to him was Nathan's dad, reading glasses sitting on the tip of his nose, wearing a chef's apron.

"There you are!" Jack said, "Ready to embark on this year's

turkey slicing ritual?"

"Absolutely," Nathan told him, stealing a quick glance at David, with whom he'd shared his concerns about his dad's lack of skill with a knife.

"I finally broke down and bought an electric carving knife."

"Oh. Well, all shiny and new, huh?" Nathan said to mask his dismay.

"Want to be the first person to try it?"

"Love to," Nathan said in grateful relief. "How do I switch it on?"

As Jack was showing Nathan how to use the knife Raymie stepped lightly into the room. David turned toward her, and Nathan and Jack looked up from the knife.

"Sorry to interrupt, but I wanted to let you know that the kids are settled down and playing a game with Marcie in the living room. Should we have them wash their hands soon?"

Jack glanced at the waiting turkey. "Let them finish the game and it will be just about time."

"Perfect," Raymie said, reaching up to give Jack a quick kiss on the cheek, which he leaned over to receive, careful not to touch her with his greasy hands.

As she left the kitchen Nathan saw his dad's admiring glance and said, "She's really lovely, Dad. You say she dances? She has that graceful, athletic look of a dancer."

"Athletic, huh? That would be a good way to put it." Jack's smile was slightly secretive, mostly smug.

David had started to laugh, but Nathan looked uncertain. "Uh, Dad, are you saying what I think you are?"

Jack burst out laughing, shoulders shaking and tears forming in the corners of his eyes from the sheer joy of it.

Nathan stared at his dad in surprise until David bumped his

shoulder with his own. "Your dad's pretty cool, Nathan."

"Well," Jack said, recovering himself a bit, "I'm sure you two know all about what it's like with new couples."

Nathan's eyes widened and David's laugh became a little nervous.

It was too weird to hear his dad talk about sex. Nathan couldn't quite get his head around it. And Jack looked so goofy in his apron with his glasses down on his nose, the blush of love on his face. Wasn't he a little too old for all of that? But what the hell, Nathan told himself, why not just be happy for him? And that thought was followed by the awareness that Jack had just included him and David in his joke (just a tad lewd there, Dad!) about new couples. So, was this his dad's way of telling them he accepted them as a couple? Nathan had wanted to ask his dad about that and was trying to figure out a way to approach the subject when he'd asked if he could invite David for Thanksgiving dinner. And here was his answer, in the simple form of a stupid joke about sex. How weird. But good. Definitely good. Pushing out a breath of relief, he told David, "Yeah, my dad's pretty cool all right."

Smiling, Nathan turned on the electric knife and got to work on the turkey while Jack took out the sweet potatoes and David poured gravy into the gravy boat. He was nearly done when Marcie strode into the kitchen.

"Well, the game's finished, Sandy's helping the kids wash up for dinner, and Stephen just carried in the pies they brought," she announced. "Is everything ready?"

"As ready as it ever will be," Jack told her.

"In that case," Marcie said, deepening her voice and raising a finger in the air, "let the nightmare begin!"

Crossing his arms, Jack said, "And when has my turkey ever

been a nightmare?"

Marcie looked at him sideways.

"Okay, there was the one time, maybe two, but that was years ago."

She continued to look at him sideways and Jack said, laughing, "Just go tell them dinner's ready."

"Hooray!" she said. "And I'm sure it's going to be scrump-sha-licious!"

"One of her infamous Marci-isms," Nathan said in response to David's questioning look, then added, "I'll explain later."

Their attention turned to Jack, who was saying, "Thanks for your vote of confidence, Marcie."

"Yeah, well, at least we know that the sweet potatoes will be good. I made those."

In response to that comment Jack pretended to kick at her and Marcie scooted out of the room, grinning broadly, arms swinging at her sides.

Jack chuckled. "She's loving this," he told Nathan and David. "You realize that she orchestrated this whole thing, inviting Raymie and her family."

"So far it seems like quite a success," Nathan told him as he put an arm around David's shoulder. David, working to contain the depth of his happiness, could only nod in agreement.

39

The last back-lit streaks of gray rode across the sky in murky contrast to the cheerful floodlights Jack had turned on so the kids could play in the backyard after dinner. Warming his hands on his coffee mug, Jack leaned against the back-porch rail as he watched the scene below him. Raymie, who had volunteered to supervise the kids, had stationed herself in the center of the yard so that she could lunge playfully at them, grunting and growling as they ran up to her and away again, squealing with joy, their mittened hands in the air, pumping short legs on bodies round with the bulk of winter coats. Raymie's grandson Aaron, the youngest of the three, was holding his own Jack thought. Stephen's girls had really taken to him and they had already made fast friends the way young children tend to do.

Jack hadn't seen Raymie dance as of yet, but her training as a dancer was evident in the effect she had created by unzipping her coat so that it would twirl as she pivoted, her hair making an arc as it whirled around her head. She crouched low, arms outstretched as she spun in circles, coat and hair flying. Standing nearly at the same height as the children as she bent to turn, she was a mixture of whirling dervish and monster whose growls were broken by laughter that came out as puffs of steam in the chill air.

"Good dinner, Dad."

Jack turned to see Stephen coming up behind him on the porch with a cup of coffee—heavy with sugar and cream—in one hand, the other hand buried in the pocket of his coat. He shivered a little. "I forgot how cold it could get here."

"A little spoiled by the California weather?" Jack said teasingly, then, "God it's good to see you again, Stephen. It's been awhile, almost a year. I hardly recognized my own granddaughters." He moved over a little so that he and Stephen could stand side by side at the porch rail.

Their attention was caught by the activity in the yard below them. Maddie, Stephen's oldest, dropped to the ground amid the last of the crinkly autumn leaves. "I'm exhausted!" she said, bringing an arm to her brow dramatically. The other two fell down beside her, laughing and panting. Raymie dropped down too, and the four of them were aligned in momentary bliss.

"That grass looks damp. They're going to get all wet," said Stephen, his voice tense with alarm.

"It's okay Stephen, Raymie's got the situation in hand. She won't let them get too mussed."

Stephen shifted his position at the rail to face his father, who continued to watch the activity in the yard. "Well, but that's the thing, Dad," he said, careful to keep his voice low, "can she really take care of them okay? I mean, how well does she see? I thought she was legally blind or something."

"She is," Jack said calmly. "She says everything is dim and blurry, but there's still a lot she can make out and she uses her other senses to fill in with what she doesn't see. Right now, I imagine that she's keeping track of the kids not only by sight, but by sound."

As they watched, Raymie stood up, brushed herself off and helped Katie, Stephen's youngest, brush the bits of yellow and red leaves from her own coat.

"So, are you pretty serious about her?" Stephen asked.

"Very," Jack said as he took a sip of his coffee that was cooling off fast, he noticed.

Raymie was helping her grandson up and Maddie started brushing leaves off his backside. He grinned at Maddie and said, "Let's play that game some more!"

Maddie looked at Raymie who bent her knees in response and began to growl. All three kids screamed in delight.

"You know, Dad, she's really nice, Sandy and I really like her, and she obviously has the kid's vote, but, I mean, are you sure you're ready to take on another person with a handicap?"

Jack turned from the scene in the yard to look at his son.

"Look, Dad," Stephen said defensively, "you already have Marcie to take care of, right?"

Regarding Stephen in annoyed surprise, Jack said, "Stephen, you grew up with Marcie. She pulled her weight in our household, including watching you boys. She's always been more of an asset than a burden. Why should that change?"

"How about when she gets older? And if you take on Raymie, too, you could end up spending the rest of your life having to take care of both of them."

Jack gave a little snort. "We really can't predict what will happen. It's just as likely that they will end up having to take care of me."

"Well, I hope that it works out for you, Dad, but I just had to tell you about my concerns. I don't want you to get into a bad situation."

"I appreciate that, Stephen. No need to worry, though—we'll be fine."

Stephen's girls had just noticed their dad on the porch and

were waving at him. Katie jumped up and down in excitement. "This is fun, Daddy! Come and play!"

Raymie stopped twirling and straightened up, looking with limited vision in the general direction of the porch, waiting to see if Stephen would join them.

"Looks like fun kids, but I'm needed in the kitchen," Stephen said.

Katie's shoulders dropped in disappointment. Jack saw this, but he wasn't sure Stephen did. But you didn't, did you, when you were a young parent and busy with other things, things that felt more important? Jack wondered how many opportunities like this he and Lisa had missed.

"I need to help your mom get dessert ready," Stephen told them. "We'll be calling you for pumpkin pie in a few more minutes."

Maddie put a hand on Katie's shoulder to console her. "Okay, Dad," she said, letting him off the hook, something Jack suspected she did often. "Yay! Pie!" she added as an afterthought before both girls turned away, their attention now on Raymie, whose playful growl resumed the game.

Stephen drained the last of his coffee. "Well, see you in a while, Dad. I don't really know how much help Sandy needs, but I'm going in where it's warm."

"She making whipped cream for the pie?"

"Wouldn't be the same without it."

"That's for sure. Let me finish my coffee and I'll be in."

After the back door clicked shut Jack stood sipping his coffee, now decidedly cold, then on impulse set the cup on the porch rail and on walked down the steps to the yard.

"Grandpa!" the girls cried out. "Are you going to play?"

"Of course!" Jack told them as three small pairs of arms

enveloped him, hugging his legs and waist according to reach, soft cheeks cuddled against the rough weave of his coat. "I wouldn't miss it for the world."

40

Spring 2014

Marcie's bedroom door was closed, but Raymie could hear the TV playing, so she rapped softly. Moments later the door was flung open by a beaming Marcie, who grabbed Raymie into a big bear hug.

"Jack must have told you," Raymie said, her voice muffled by Marcie's shoulder.

Releasing her grip on Raymie, Marcie stepped back to look into her face. "He sure as heck did! I'm so happy!"

"Oh good. I thought you would be." Raymie's voice changed tone. "Listen, Marcie, we've been talking about selling my house and living here. Is that going to work for you?"

"Of course it is! Jack already asked me about that and I said I thought that was perfect. Only thing is, do you two want to have this room here in the house? I'd kind of like to move back into my old apartment again."

"Oh! I hadn't thought of that. Let me talk it over with Jack. I imagine he'll be in favor of the idea."

"Yeah, I'm sure we'll figure it out. The main thing is that we're all gonna be together!"

"I know! It's going to be wonderful." Raymie paused. "Marcie, there was something I especially wanted to ask you about."

"What's that?"

"Well, Jack's brother Steve is going to stand up with him and I'd like you to be the one who stands up with me, if you're willing."

"You mean like be your maid of honor? Sure! I'm an old hand at that. I was Lisa's maid of honor, you know. Will we be wearing garlands in our hair like we did then, and long dresses?"

"Well, we're thinking about a fairly small wedding, so I imagine we'll want to wear nice dresses of some kind, but nothing too formal."

"How about hats? We should wear hats."

"What a great idea! Something vintage could be fun. I wonder if we can get Jack to wear a top hat. Or maybe a bowler. He'd look very handsome in a bowler."

"Okay! And we'll have dancing too!"

"Oh, yes! Certainly we'll dance, Marcie."

"Yay!" Marcie said, giving Raymie another hug. "I get to dance with my new sister!"

"Sister?"

Marcie stood looking at Raymie, hands on hips.

"Oh! You mean me! I guess we will be sisters of a sort."

Damn betcha we will!

Tears sprang to Raymie's eyes.

"You okay, Rainy?"

"Oh yes, Marcie, I'm fine. I'm just happy. You see, I've never had a sister before."

"Aw, Rainy, you were my sister from the first time I met you!"

41
Greece, 20th Anniversary

The Aegean Sea. The name sounded so ancient.
Raymie breathed in the salty scent. The waves were quiet this morning, their ebb and flow soft and simple, devoid of the dramatic crash of the night before. Leaning lightly on her cane, Raymie removed her sandals, silver hair falling over her cheeks as she bent side to side. Her bare feet gingerly tested the sand, which she found delightfully smooth and warm.
Turning her face toward the horizon, she could make out the low dark forms of the nearby islands, the glint of sun on the waves, the light expanse of the sky . . . little else. But that was enough. Jack had said there were fishing boats on the water and described them so she could imagine what they looked like, comparing them to the memories of all the boats she had seen in her lifetime, how they were different and how they were the same.
The quiet lap of waves was punctuated by the cries of shore birds and the waft of conversation from down the beach, the rise and fall of a language she didn't quite recognize. There were some muted sounds somewhere behind her where she imagined Jack was wandering, looking for shells.
A little breeze lifted the edge of the light tunic she wore over her shorts, and moved wisps of hair across her face, coaxing her

into the water, to feel the soft churn of waves around her ankles.

Raymie stepped in. The water was warm, so unlike the Pacific, the ocean she'd known her entire life, which was cold even in the heat of summer. The wave that pushed around her feet was sensually smooth. She dug her toes in the sand as it pulled away again, creating a hollow where she stood, the tiny grains moving across her skin, flowing forward, deeper into the sea.

Raymie sighed with quiet joy.

This vacation had been a good idea. They were uncertain at first; Raymie in the later years of her seventh decade, was still lithe and energetic, still dancing, though not at the level she once did. Jack, at eighty-one, had recently survived a heart attack, and though his doctor had encouraged him to take this trip, they were still anxious about his health.

But the kids, Raymie's Allison and Jack's Nathan and Stephen, had urged them to go. It was, after all, their twentieth anniversary, so Raymie and Jack put their anxieties aside to fulfill a mutual dream to visit Greece.

The long flight there was a trial, as they expected it to be, hard on old constitutions. To take their minds from the discomfort, Jack had read his favorite passages from "The Iliad" to Raymie, who listened to the rhythm of his voice, enthralled by the beauty of the lines and comforted by the easy press of his shoulder against hers.

Jack was walking toward her. He too carried a cane, a concession to old age. She could hear the thump as he moved it at his side, careful to shield his arthritic knees from strain.

As Jack drew close, he said quietly, "Look at this, Rainy!"

She held out her hand, palm up, and he placed the object in the center, a shell.

"Here, let me take those," he said, taking her sandals and cane so she could use both hands to explore the shell. Her fingers running across the rough whorls on the outside, she then discovered the satiny inside.

"Oh! It's lovely!" she murmured, her fingers tracing the curved edge.

Jack turned to look out at the water. "This is so beautiful." He gazed a moment longer before emitting a little tired sigh.

"Are you ready to head back for lunch?" she asked him.

"Maybe a short nap first."

"That sounds good to me. And I'll put in a call to Marcie when we get back to the hotel. I want to hear how Diva is doing."

"I'm sure she's doing fine. Probably getting spoiled to death. Marcie is the consummate dog sitter."

"Oh, I know, it's just that Diva's getting so old and I worry about her. Do you realize that she's nearly the age Shainy was when she died?"

"Is that right, Raymie? I hadn't realized that. Of course you'd want to check on her."

Sitting in the padded rattan chair in their hotel room, Raymie said goodbye to Marcie and handed the phone to Jack so he could end the call for her.

"Marcie's doing well," she told Jack, even though she was certain he had heard both sides of the conversation. "And Diva's fine. Marcie said Maddie was in Seattle for a few days and took the ferry over to find out if Marcie needed anything."

"That was nice of her," Jack said as he lowered himself onto the bed with a slight groan. "Stephen's raised himself a responsible girl there."

"Not really that much of a girl anymore. She turned twenty-eight in October."

"God, is she that old already? Well, but she still seems like a kid to me." Jack pushed one of his shoes off with his other foot and it made a clop as it hit the floor, then pushed off the other.

"Marcie said Maddie wished us a happy anniversary and said she's sorry she couldn't come for the party."

"That was nice of her," Jack said with a yawn. His voice slowed. "Twenty years. Can you believe it, Rainy girl?"

"I know. It's really something."

"Happiest years of my life," Jack said sleepily.

Raymie got up from the chair and moved along the edge of the bed, her fingers skimming the curved ridges of the embossed bedspread until she found her way to the side opposite Jack. She bent down to slip off her shoes, then swung her legs onto the bed next to Jack, stretching her legs to the tips of her toes, then scooting down so that she could stretch her arms above her, linking her fingers to flex them. She sighed, contented. "What a lovely room this is. I don't really care that it's so small, do you?"

"Not at all. This seems a lot more like how I had imagined a hotel room in Greece would be. Kind of a romanticized idea, I suppose, but if we'd taken the hotel the kids wanted us to have, we may as well have been in the States."

"They meant well," Raymie said, absently running her stockinged foot along his calf.

Jack reached out and took her hand, his thumb caressing the tips of her fingers. So small, so soft. "Hey, Rainy?"

"Hmm?"

"Do you think it's true what they say about foreign environments being, um, stimulating?"

"Stimulating? You mean intellectually or . . ."

"No, I mean the other kind of stimulating."

Raymie rolled to her side and propped her head up with a hand. "Really, Jack?" she said a hint of laughter in her voice. "I mean, I love the idea!" Then turning serious she said, "But what about your heart?"

"Oh, screw my damn heart! Last appointment with Doctor Rosen, she said I was doing a lot better."

Raymie set her chin on his chest, her eyes looking up into his face. "Screw your heart, huh? It may have been awhile, but I do seem to recall that the area of interest was a bit lower down," she said deftly.

"Rainy!" He tried to look shocked as she batted her eyes innocently at him.

Their shared laughter was soft and followed by an embarrassed hesitation before they moved cautiously, gently, together. Jack had a moment of panic, fearing he'd be clumsy or worse, but Raymie took charge, her lovemaking the sublime choreography it had always been.

Lying together side by side in the aftermath, Jack, feeling completely at peace, watched as the afternoon sun made flickering patterns on the ceiling over their heads.

"Wow," he said. "I'd forgotten just exactly how wonderful sex can be." He glanced over at Raymie. "And I had quite honestly believed that that part of our life together was over. That we were just too old for such nonsense."

"Apparently not," Raymie said, her voice soft and dreamy.

"You never know," Jack told her. "Just when you think, 'That's it, you'll never do that again,' life steps forward and says 'surprise!' I imagine there's a lot of truth in the saying, 'it's not over 'til it's over.' Maybe there's no such thing as the last time for anything." He was silent for a moment. "No, that's not right—of course there will be a last time. We just can't predict when that will be."

Raymie rolled to her stomach. "I guess the most important thing is now. That we're here together now and are aware of how wonderful this time together is."

"It's pretty amazing, isn't it?" Jack said, his voice becoming heavy with sleep.

"Pretty amazing, all right."

Raymie leaned over to kiss his cheek and saw that Jack had already drifted off. "I love you so much, Jack," she whispered, smiling into his sleeping face.

She patted him on his shoulder and rolled over onto her back, closed her eyes, still smiling.

42

UNDER A VAST CLOUDLESS SKY, so very, very blue, the ephemeral air danced around her in tiny dots of light. She watched her bare feet, pale as goldfish, swish lazily through softly rolling waves.

Somewhere out there the patter of rain started up, became louder.

Rain? That didn't fit. Puzzled, she turned to Jack, who nodded, his gentle smile assuring her that all was just as it should be.

Raymie opened her eyes. She was home, sitting in her worn leather armchair, the afghan that Allison had made her a few Christmases back tucked around her knees. Above her, she heard the drum of raindrops on the roof.

It came to her that she'd been dreaming about being in Greece. That was quite a while ago, the trip to Greece—almost nine years now.

Marcie, sitting in the chair next to hers, teased, "Well, sleepy head, did you have a nice nap?"

Raymie smiled sheepishly. She'd been nodding off a lot lately. "Did I snore?"

"Not really. You were just asleep for a little while."

Raymie listened to the drumming on the roof. "Has it been

raining very long?"

"No, just started a few minutes ago."

"It seems to be slowing down now."

"Yeah."

Raymie heard Marcie settle in her chair and the rustle of a magazine, then, "Hey look, Rainy, it's snowing!"

"Is it?" Raymie said, leaning forward, "Oh yes! I might just be able to see some flakes against the dark of the hedge." But she realized that was probably wishful thinking. She really couldn't see the snow, just sense it by the scent in the air and the drop in temperature.

Raymie moved the afghan aside to get up from her chair and went out to the covered porch. She stretched a hand beyond the edge of the roof to feel the flakes. "The snow's kind of wet," Raymie reported to Marcie as she came back in. "It'll probably turn to rain later." She sat down and picked up her audio book from the side table that sat between their two chairs.

After a few minutes, Raymie paused the recording. "Is it raining again? I think I hear raindrops."

"Yeah, it's raining. No, wait, there's some snow mixed in with it." Marcie was silent as she looked out the window for a few moments. "Yay! It's snowing again!"

Raymie settled back in her chair. Sighed. "Jack used to love days like this. He'd have his nose in a book most of the day, drinking coffee, and later he'd make us a big dinner. Comfort food like fried chicken, mashed potatoes and gravy."

"And you'd make the salad."

"And I'd make the salad."

Marcie glanced over at Raymie to see if she was crying, then nodded to herself, satisfied that she was fine, she was remembering Jack in a happy way.

Raymie reached across the side table to give Marcie's hand a little squeeze. "Thank you for bringing me into the family, Marcie."

"You mean like so you could meet Jack?"

"Yes, like that."

"Aw, that was a long time ago."

"Yes, but I'm still so grateful."

Marcie sat looking at the snow. "We're pretty old now, aren't we Rainy."

"I'd certainly say so!"

Marcie struggled out of her chair and shuffled past where Raymie was seated. "Want some hot chocolate?"

"That sounds tempting, but didn't your doctor say you shouldn't have sweets?"

"Oh, I know, but let's make it special just for today. Because of the snow."

"Okay, Marcie, a special treat because of the snow."

Before she started her slow trek to the kitchen, Marcie took a moment to lean over and place a kiss the top of Raymie's head.

Smiling, Raymie reached to turn on her audiobook, then changing her mind she set it down again and leaned back against the headrest to listen to the sound of Marcie putting water on to boil, opening the cupboard to get out the mix, and setting two mugs on the counter. Tasks she had performed hundreds of times that held the comfort of home, the repeated rituals that make up a life.

As she listened Raymie let the soul of the house curl around her. She felt the reverberations of voices, the pulse of footsteps both hurried and halted, the grief, the alliances and conflicts, the hilarity and joy. And within this flow of shared lives she found tranquility, a steadiness, like the gentle lap of water along a shore.

"Here's your hot chocolate, Rainy. I added a little milk last minute so it's not too hot."

Raymie reached out to accept the mug held before her. Cupping it in her hands, she took a small sip.

"Thank you, Marcie. This is perfect."

She took another sip as Marcie set her own mug on the side table and moved heavily into her chair.

As they sat side by side Raymie heard her own contentment echoed in Marcie's sigh as each nestled deeper into her chair. They settled into comfortable silence, the snow falling softly around them.

Acknowledgements

I owe an equal debt of gratitude to Linda Finnegan and Marci Peterson. Marci for starting our writer's group, and unfailingly providing me with the encouragement I needed to keep going, even when I lost faith. Her suggestions for revision were always spot-on, and her ability to push me to develop my skills as a writer were beyond value. What she has taught me about writing could fill a book!

A million thanks to Linda Finnigan for taking on the exhausting role of editor and proofreader. A truly good friend, her sometimes harsh criticism made her praise and excitement as the book took shape all the more valuable. From the time I first began the book, Linda has brought my characters to life through her readings, helping me to hear what passages worked, and which needed to be altered.

I owe a big thank you to Mark Peterson and Geoff Dugwyler for their dedication to the difficult task of formatting this book. Mark, a talented poet, has also been of great assistance in revising and refining the poetry within these pages. And kudos to Angela Tanabe for the many hours she put in to the cover design.

I want to thank all the members of my writer's group, both past and present for their support and patience through countless revisions: Marci, Anna, Mark, Linda, Tom, Jane, Barbara, and Walter.

The character of Marcie is based on the men and women

who experience cognitive challenges that I've been so fortunate to have known throughout my lifetime. You have enriched my life in so many ways. Thank you for the important lessons you have taught me, and the love you've sent my way.

And lastly, I want to thank my husband Bruce for enduring my many hours at the computer and for being my most valued critic.

Acknowledgement of resources

Lise Solvang of Fiber and Clay, a dance student for many years, for her correction and confirmation of the passages related to the experiences of a young student of dance.

Kyle Parrish for sharing the everyday life of a person using the service of a guide dog, and his stories about his wonderful guide dog Peter, who though he is no longer with us, was such a delight to all who knew him.

Cheryl Thompson MS, CCC, SLP, of Sound Speech and Language for teaching me about her profession and for sharing her experiences from the many years she has done this important work.

About the Author

A native of Washington state, Bess Hendrick lives on the Olympic Peninsula with her husband, two dogs and a cat. *Welcoming the Rain* is her first novel.

Made in United States
Troutdale, OR
04/19/2024